THE
GREEN-EYED
GUARDIAN

JOEY CARDONA

THE
GREEN-EYED
GUARDIAN

THE FALLEN HEROES REBORN ● BOOK 1

The Green-Eyed Guardian by Joey Cardona
Copyright © 2021 by Joey Cardona
All Rights Reserved.
ISBN: 978-1-59755-638-5

Published by: ADVANTAGE BOOKS™
                  Longwood, FL
                  www.advbookstore.com

Library of Congress Catalog Number: 2021937590

Names: Cardona, Joey, Author

Title: The Green-Eyed Guardian / Joey Cardona

Description   Longwood: Advantage Books, 2021

Identifiers: ISBN Print: 9781597556385
                  ePub: 9781597556587
                  Subjects: Fiction, Fantasy

First Printing: May 2021
21 22 23 24 25 26   10 9 8 7 6 5 4 3 2 1

1

The Survivor

"What happened to me?"

Fire rained down from the evening sky, casting streaks of light across the soldier's armor. Battle cries were heard over the sounds of swords and shields clashing. The thunderous crash of falling stone, as walls collapsed and buildings crumbled, was deafening. The soldier looked around in confusion, seeing the bodies of his fallen comrades. Holding his chest, breathing heavily, his eyes darting around looking for signs of life. He sat in a sea of corpses, trying to process what he was seeing. Realizing his armor felt odd under his fingers, he looked down to find a bloody gash in the leather protecting his heart. "What? No time... I need to find survivors..." Chronol quickly picked up his sword and shield and rushed to a nearby building, remembering that he had helped people hide there before the battle. He burst through the door and immediately stopped in his tracks; the wavering light of burning structures entered the doorway from behind him, piercing the darkness of the room and illuminating the bodies of women and children lying in red pools throughout the room.

"No... not them, too..." he whispered, falling to his knees. "Anyone...? Is anyone alive?" He called into the room. His question was met with only silence. The sound of metal rattled softly as his shield trembled against the stone floor, his hand shaking while tears fell from his eyes. "Why...? Why...?" He stood up and walked back into the street. The sounds of combat still echoed from the far side of town. "They're still fighting..." Taking a deep breath, he gripped his sword tightly and started walking in the direction of the shouting. Suddenly, a loud crack of lightning overhead made him stop in his tracks. He looked up to see a massive red dragon plummeting from the sky. It tumbled limply through the air before crashing into a building in front of him. The ground shook from the impact as Chronol gasped at the sight. "Kaaldoth! Kaaldoth… has fallen?" He said, looking down at the ground, reeling from the shock. "If Kaaldoth has fallen… then all hope is lost. We've… lost…" He looked up into the sky again, seeing winged creatures flying around, crying out in pain as bolts of lightning picked them off one by one.

Looking once again towards the battle cries, then south to the gate, he stood for a moment. With tears streaming down his face, he sheathed his sword and whispered painfully, "…I'm sorry." Keeping to the shadows amid the debris, he began quietly heading south. Along the way, he heard a noise from around the corner of a building. Peeking carefully down the alley, it appeared no one was there. He proceeded to search the alleyway until he heard the sound of soft whimpering coming from a crate near the wall. Approaching cautiously, he looked behind it, finding a small, trembling wolfhound pup. "Maksis!" he cried, putting his hand out and beckoning for the small animal. "C'mere, boy. It's ok. Come on, we're getting out of here." Seeing the familiar face, it crawled closer, trying to climb into the outstretched hand. Chronol carefully scooped up the hound, holding him close, and continued to the outer gate. Once close enough to survey the situation, Chronol realized there were Kohtan soldiers stationed at the exit, waiting to stop survivors from escaping. "Not a good idea…" he thought to himself. He was a Thoron soldier, and so, even outnumbered, he knew he had the advantage in melee combat, but having to fight while keeping Maksis safe at the same time was not a risk he was willing to take.

"I'll get you out of here, little one. Don't worry," Chronol whispered reassuringly. He carefully snuck through back alleys, getting closer to the wall south of the gate. The tall, stone structures provided shadow for him to pass under, darting from building to building. "This should be far enough…" he thought, looking at the house adjacent to the wall. With unnatural height he jumped towards the wall, kicking off it and scaling the side of the building.

Landing lightly on the roof, he was careful not to make noise and draw attention. From this new vantage point, he could see more of the town in ruin. His heart sank, seeing his home burning just a few streets away. Chronol looked down at the little life in his arms and took a deep breath. Facing the wall, he backed up and with a running start, leapt towards the wall. Beginning to fall short, he reached his free hand up and just barely caught the ledge. Dangling from his fingertips, he slowly pulled himself up, climbing onto the outer wall. Careful not to be seen, he peeked down below to ensure there were no soldiers nearby. With the way clear and Maksis safely tucked close to his chest, Chronol jumped down from the wall out of the city and landed on the ground in a roll. Quickly getting up he made a mad dash for the treeline. In a few moments he was safely in the woods and wasted no time running south, constantly glancing over his shoulder watching for pursuers.

After running far enough to lose sight of the city, he finally stopped to catch his breath, finding himself surrounded by nothing more than the sounds of nature. Critters scurried around in the brush as a breeze rustled the leaves nearby, carrying the scent of smoke through the woods. Finally having a moment without immediate danger, the soldier remembered the wound in his chest. He peered into his damaged armor, but to his surprise there was no injury to be seen. "That's odd…" Chronol thought to himself, still too on edge to question the situation further, listening for enemy soldiers. He started making his way East, hoping to get around the invading army and end up behind them, pushing through the night to take advantage of as much darkness as possible before daybreak. He decided to find a place to rest when the dim light of the sun began to rise. Afraid of being found by a patrol, he climbed high up into a tree and laid back on a thick branch to rest. Loosening his chest armor, he slipped Maksis inside to keep him from wandering off and possibly falling. With the adrenaline wearing off, he was overtaken by exhaustion and passed out.

Fire rained down from the evening sky, casting streaks of light across the soldier's armor. Battle cries mixed with the clashing sounds of swords and shields. The thunderous crash of falling stone, as walls collapsed and buildings crumbled, was deafening. Piercing through the chaos was the sound of a child crying. "What're you doing out here? You need to get inside NOW!" the soldier cried out. The child looked at him, tears streaming from his eyes; a small, wooden toy horse clutched in his hand. The boy opened his mouth to scream, but no sound came out.

Chronol's eyes opened suddenly as he gasped. He looked around quickly, heart pounding in his ears in time with his rapid breathing, taking in the branches and leaves surrounding him. Realizing it was just a dream, he sat back against the tree holding his forehead. The soldier reached for his chest, once again feeling the gash in his armor. "It was real…" he looked up and sighed. "What on earth happened last night?" A small tongue licked the tip of his finger. Looking back down at his armour, he remembered tucking Maksis in there the night before. "Hey there, little guy," he smiled and pulled the pup from his hiding place. "You sleep alright?" The little black wolfhound climbed gently up his chest, staring at him with brown and silver eyes, its tiny tail gently wagging. Chronol scratched his back, holding him like a baby. "Least I still have you," he said, closing his eyes to get some more rest.

They rested there together for another hour or so before Chronol finally had the energy to get up. Putting Maksis safely back in his armor, he climbed to the top of the tree to get a better view of his surroundings. His jaw fell slack at what lay beyond the canopy of the trees. The sun shone like a spotlight, with his hometown sitting center stage. A pillar of black smoke danced up from the obscured flames in the ruined city. Black armored soldiers continued to march into Thoros, their machines of war encircling the northeastern border. "We need to get as far away from here as possible," Chronol thought to himself. He worked his way back down to the forest floor below. Traveling southeast, he kept to a slower, quieter pace than before. Birds tweeting, squirrels climbing, crickets chirping, leaves rustling; his senses were on high alert, taking in every little sound as he watched for Kohtan soldiers.

When the sun began its descent, he was distracted by a grumbling sound. "Hmm…" he thought, holding his hand to his stomach, "we're gonna need food." Maintaining his course, he began searching, looking for any signs of wildlife that could be a meal. After a short while, he picked up on a set of small tracks and followed them. A little ways further a rabbit was peeking up through the grass. He kept out of sight and quietly pulled a knife from the back of his belt. Taking aim, he waited for the rabbit to settle into a new position before throwing the knife. The blade pierced its body, killing it instantly. Smiling, he approached his kill and withdrew the blade before carefully skinning the fluffy creature till only fresh meat remained. Removing Maksis from his armor, he placed him in front of the food. "Eat up, little one. This one's yours." He smiled, watching the little black ball of fur pounce on the rabbit, as if to keep it from escaping. Its tiny teeth tore at the meat while his little paws pinned it down.

Chronol tossed the blade up, catching it flipped over to change his grip. "Hmm… there's probably another one around here somewhere," he thought, looking around for more signs of life. He waited for Maksis to finish eating before continuing his hunt. Sniffing the air, he crept through the brush until hearing a rustle nearby. He froze, looking for the source of the disturbance. His eyes locked onto a similar prey as it poked its long, brown ears out of the grass. Without hesitation, he threw his knife at the creature, slaying it just as fast as the last. The soldier collected his quarry and began picking up a few pieces of wood, stone and tinder. After checking for any nearby patrols, he sat his weaponry against a nearby tree and started a small fire. While Maksis hopped around in the grass, he skinned and cooked the small creature then devoured the meal, thankful for the bounty the forest had provided.

"I was more hungry than I realized," he sighed, leaning back against a tree. Maksis quickly jumped into his lap, tail wagging happily. "You're recovering well from all this," he said scratching behind the pup's ears. "We're on the run you know. There's no telling where other soldiers may be, we need to get as far away from town as possible." The tiny wolf barked, almost as if responding to his master's concerns. Thoughts stirred and echoed in the back of his head. "What am I doing…? I'm running away from the only home I've ever known… A city I was sworn to protect… I should've stayed and fought… Why did I run? I could've helped…" These thoughts swelled in his mind until they were interrupted by a snapping sound to the west.

His vision darted in that direction, immediatly finding the source of the disturbance. He grabbed Maksis and rolled away a split second before a bolt whistled through the air and planted into the tree he had been resting against. Four Kohtan soldiers emerged from the woods, one wielding a crossbow while the others brandished swords and an axe. Chronol quickly tucked his four-legged companion behind a tree and made a break for his weaponry but was cut off by a Kohtan soldier. The soldier swung his sword at the unarmed Thoron, only to find his weapon stopped short; his wrist tightly gripped by Chronol, who proceeded to punch his attacker in the face, sending him tumbling to the ground. With the obstacle removed from his path, Chronol swiftly grabbed his sword and shield, immediately attacking the downed soldier before he could get his bearings. His sword sliced through its target like a hot knife through butter, severing the man's torso in two. The other soldiers stared wide-eyed at the sight.

"That's a Thoron all right," one of them said to the others. They charged in and the aforementioned Thoron rushed to meet them. The one brandishing a sword moved to the right as the other flanked from the opposite direction. Chronol readied himself, preparing for an attack from either side. It came first from the swordsman, whose blade he deflected with his own glimmering sword. The other followed suit, swinging his axe which was stopped cold by Chronol's hearty shield. Chronol stepped towards the swordsman, letting the axe wielder fall forward and lose his balance. He spun around, bringing his shield into the swordsman's face while thrusting his sword into the other soldier's chest. Blood spilled to the floor, followed quickly by an axe as the Kohtan's grip went limp. Meanwhile, the archer was rushing to reload his crossbow. Seeing that the bow was almost loaded, Chronol kicked the dead soldier off of his blade, then turned around and stabbed the dazed swordsman. Grabbing him, Chronol moved the impaled soldier's body between himself and the archer. He shoved the dying fiend into the bowman, knocking the crossbow from his hands. Dashing forward, he quickly dispatched his remaining attackers.

"They attacked without warning," he said, taking a deep breath. "Maks?" he called out, looking back towards where the pup had been hidden. A little black ball of fur stood next to the tree growling, looking ready to pounce. "It's ok, little one," Chronol laughed softly. "They're not getting up. Come," he called, kneeling down. The little wolfhound bounced through the tall grass, leaping into his master's embrace. "Good boy. You showed them." Cradling the pup, he kicked sand into the fire until it was out.

They headed east, unsure of their destination, only knowing that they needed to stay on the move and get away from the army. "No warning... Not a word..." he thought to himself. "Who just fires at someone blindly without finding out who they are? Do they have orders to kill on sight? What if I wasn't a Thoron? Are they just that savage that anyone that isn't one of their soldiers is an acceptable casualty? Maybe that group was just overzealous.... But I can't take a chance on that. Best keep hidden from any patrols, it doesn't seem likely that I'll be able to just wander by like a normal traveller if they're that on edge. This armor isn't helping me blend in either." Chronol had decided against using a cloak from the Kohtan soldiers as a disguise, concerned another Thoron survivor might see him and attack, thinking he was the enemy. He continued going over the events of the day in his mind, trying to gauge the level of danger, figuring out where to go and the best route to avoid more soldiers.

A few hours later, the sun began to creep down behind the horizon. Chronol had been careful to avoid the two patrols he had encountered along the way, staying in the brush and giving them a wide berth. Being in a constant state of high alert was very taxing so he would need to sleep soon. Finding another tall, thick tree to use, he climbed up into the branches to sleep in relative safety. Pulling Maks back out of his armor, he pet him softly as the pup laid on his lap. "What are we going to do, little one...?" he asked his now napping companion. "Are we going to be constantly on the run like this? Is this our life now? Are we all that's left? That can't be, can it? Zerahl was a master swordsman, even better than I. I can't imagine someone besting him, even ten to one. He... he probably escaped like I did... surely I'm not the only survivor." Chronol continued his one-sided conversation with the sleeping wolf until he could no longer keep his eyes open. Gently tucking Maksis safely into his armor, he let sleep take him, leaving those worries for tomorrow's Chronol to deal with.

2

The Fugitive

Battle cries were heard over the sounds of swords and shields clashing. Piercing through the chaos was the sound of a child crying. "What're you doing out here? You need to get inside NOW!" the soldier cried out. The child looked at him, tears streaming from his eyes; a small, wooden toy horse clutched in his hand. The boy screamed but no sound came out. Chronol's eyes grew wide as he reached out, time seeming to slow down as a cold, iron ballista bolt crept through the air, growing closer to the boy.

"DARAN!" Chronol shouted as he suddenly sat up, his trembling hand outstretched to grab the boy that was no longer there. A tiny bark emanated from his chest. Maksis was peeking out of his armor, awoken by his master's sudden outburst. He breathed heavily, almost hyperventilating. The dawn sun tinted the leaves swaying gently around him.

"Did you hear that?" a gravelly voice said in the distance. Chronol quickly covered his mouth and pressed back against the tree. His vision scanned the direction the voice came from, looking for signs of movement.

"I think it came from this way…" another voice spoke up. Maksis let out a soft growl but was promptly quieted by his master. Looking on, he noticed six figures emerging from the foliage. Chronol remained motionless, a bead of sweat slowly running down the side of his face. The men, wearing typical black and gold Kohtan military armor, stalked through the forest, hunting the source of the sound they heard. They made their way closer until they were directly beneath Chronol, stopping next to his tree. He carefully reached out and pulled a small nut from the tree, looking for a gap through the branches.

Seeing a small opening, he threw the acorn to the north, bouncing it against another tree and into a bush. The soldiers quickly turned towards the direction of the sound. A squirrel suddenly emerged from the bush holding the nut. The small rodent squeaked at the soldiers, then scurried up the nearby tree with its bounty between its teeth. "Stupid rat…" one of the soldiers groaned as they sheathed their weapons.

"You were scared, weren't you," one of the others teased.

"Fool, as if I would be afraid of a squirrel," he replied.

"You were afraid it was a Thoron, weren't you? You should've seen the fear in your eyes. Some leader you are. I should just kill you and take command of this squad." It seemed as if that comment lit a fire in his leader's eyes. The muscular commander grabbed his insulting subordinate by the throat, pinning him to a tree with one hand, slowly drawing his blade with the other. He reached up and rested the sharp edge on the struggling soldier's throat, moving it slightly until a drop of blood leaked out.

"If you ever… EVER disrespect me that way again, it'll be the last mistake you make in your pitiful excuse for a life. No Thoron scares me, I don't care how many patrols they cut apart. We'll find them, and we'll end them, even if I have to do it alone. The Overlord bids it and so it shall be done." He released his powerful grip from the now slightly blue soldier, letting him fall to his knees coughing and gasping for air. "Pick yourself up and let's move out. We have Thorons to hunt."

The soldiers moved out, one of them helping his coughing ally to his feet. Chronol remained motionless, staring off into the distance as they left. "They… he said THEY…" he thought to himself. "Thorons… not A THORON but THORONS… I knew I wasn't the only survivor." His heart skipped a beat at the thought of being reunited with any of his people. "I need to find them. Where could they be hiding? Where would they be heading?" He pondered for a few minutes, trying to figure out how he'd find the other survivors. "I… I need to go back, don't I… My best chance to find them is to find some trail where they escaped from the city and follow them from there… That means heading back into the mouth of the beast…" He took a deep breath and tightly gripped the pommel of this sword. "If that's what it takes to find them… then so be it. Maks, we're going home."

With newfound determination he climbed down from the tree and headed west, back towards Thoros; the home he had left in fire and ruin. His pace heading back was quick at first, thinking of the other survivors that might be found there. He wondered who else might have survived, how they escaped, how many there were. But as his memory flashed back to the state his home was in when he left, his pace slowed. Images of the city in flames weighed him down, slowing each step. He stopped and leaned against a tree for a moment, feeling a knot twisting around in his stomach. His eyes watered at the thought of seeing his home in that state again. It had been days since he saw his home, who knew what was left of it. With the amount of destructive force the Kohtans brought to their doorstep, the entire city could be dust and cinders by now. But he refused to let himself believe his city was gone. Wiping his eyes and continuing on, he prepared himself for what was to come. It took a couple days of backtracking through the woods and avoiding patrols to reach the outskirts of Thoros.

Unfortunately, nothing could have prepared him for this. The fires he last saw had finally been put out and the smoke had cleared. Adorning the tall walls of his once beautiful city were black and gold Kohtan banners. On both sides of each banner was a rope dangling down, and at the end of each rope was a body. The corpses of his dead brethren were displayed around the city, a show of power and conquest. The bodies of dragons laid scattered outside of town, resting in the craters they made from falling out of the sky. Chronol's jaw hung agape, his lips quivering and his eyes filling with tears. He fell to his knees, sobbing and looking on in shock as the tears spilled over. Leaning back against a tree, holding his knees to his chest, he stared at the horror surrounding his home. Seconds seemed like hours as he tried to absorb the images in front of him. He was too far away to make out the faces of the people on the wall, but close enough to recognize some of the dragons. These were majestic creatures that had lived alongside the Thorons in peace. Creatures that had taken it upon themselves to protect this land that they called home. And now they lay beside the civilization they had chosen, loved, and protected; the two that much closer to extinction.

Eventually, he dried his face and built up the courage to continue, reminding himself there were others out there that needed his help. He refused to let any more of his people suffer the same fate. Chronol carefully headed back to the area where he escaped from and observed the soldiers nearby. It seemed most of the army had made its way inside and was occupying Thoros. Some guards could be seen leaving the city, carrying the bodies of the Thorons that fell during the attack and throwing them into a mass grave. Chronol sat in the nearby treeline watching them come and go. Sitting on a branch, looking down at the bodies, he stared on for hours, looking at the different familiar faces; the old fisherman he always bought salmon from, the blonde girl from the flower shop that always smiled at him when he walked by, the young guard in training that he was instructing, his neighbor's son that always played near his home, barely eight years old. Memories of all these people flowed through his mind as he scanned the corpses for loved ones.

"They were innocent. Most of these people weren't even soldiers. Women, children, the elderly. Do these Kohtans have no shame? No conscience? No morals or standards? Why did they even attack us?" He thought to himself. Pausing for a moment, he realized he had no answer to that question. "Why DID they attack us? We've done nothing to them. Certainly, we've seen their patrols and know of their conquests, but Kohtans have always conquered to conscript more land and fighters into their army. They didn't even warn us. No ultimatum, no demands, no messenger, nothing. They just showed up at our doorstep apparently set on wiping out our entire people. This wasn't some attack on a whim. They came with such destructive force that they even had enough to take down the dragons protecting the city. This was planned, thought out, prepared for. Why?? What did we do to spark their aggression? We've never attacked their patrols, never tried to encroach on their territory, never done anything to pose a threat to them aside from simply existing. Everyone knows Thorons train in combat for the purpose of better disciplining ourselves and training our bodies and minds. We have no ambitions of moving into their territory and starting a war. What was their purpose? If this was about acquiring new blood for their army, why did they try to kill everyone off? Why kill a race of warriors who have dedicated their lives to mastering the art of combat? Any Thoron man is worth ten or twenty of their soldiers in combat, why waste that resource? I don't understand! What did they want from us?"

He gripped his head in frustration, trying to understand why this tragedy befell his people. A soft whimper came from his chest as Maksis peeked his head out of the hole in his armor. Chronol pulled the pup out and held him close. "It's ok, Maks, I'll be alright. I just don't understand, little one. Why did they do this to us?" The hound nuzzled his master's neck, placing his paws on Chronol's shoulder. "...why..." his mind continued. "We have no riches or vast lands or great treasures hidden away. The most valuable thing in Thoros was the dragons and those too were killed. It'll take years to repair the damage they've done to the city. For what purpose? What good did this do them? What did they hope to obtain? They always want something, but we had nothing unusually valuable so we thought ourselves safe. Anything in our lands we would have happily shared, so what sense would it make to attack us?" Unanswerable questions continued to plague him for what felt like forever.

Finally, at sunset, the soldiers stopped delivering bodies, leaving only two guards near the gate. Chronol took the opportunity to get closer, avoiding the sight of the posted guards. He cautiously made his way around the city, looking for any tracks of escaped survivors. This proved more difficult than he'd hoped considering he had waited till dusk before beginning his search. Nothing stood out to him until he got around to the northern side of the city. There he found a lone set of boot prints heading away from the city. He followed the trail, excited to have finally found something. The tracks led into the woods where he found a soldier squatting near a tree. His garb was that of the Kohtan army so Chronol hid himself and waited. The Kohtan cleaned himself and headed back towards the city. Upon closer inspection, Chronol realized the tracks he was following belonged to the guard he had just watched relieve himself in the woods. Disheartened, he headed back and finished his search, but to no avail. Any tracks of people escaping had long since been muddled by the invading army and patrols. Coming full circle back to the mass grave where he started, the soldier was unsure what to do next.

"Kaerill… Kaerill's not there…" he thought, mentally going over the faces he saw in the grave. "Wait, she had a cousin trading with merchants in Eppildor when the attack happened. Maybe she ran there to hide with him? What was his name? …I can't remember. I should go search there, maybe I'll find them." He looked down at his bloody armor, putting his finger through the hole near his chest, scratching Maksis' nose. "I'm going to have to change my clothes if I want to have a chance at blending in." He looked at the mass grave, searching the bodies for someone his size. All the right size candidates had blood streaked across their clothing. He realized that in order to blend in, he'd need a clean outfit, but the only clean clothes he knew of were in town. His only options were to continue with his bloody armor or try to sneak back into the city to find a clean set of clothes. "This is going to be the most dangerous laundry run of my life…" he grinned, almost laughing. He picked up several small stones and crept near the gate guards. Quietly getting as close as he could, he threw one of the stones into the treeline in front of them. Their attention shifted focus towards the sound. While they squinted into the darkness, trying to see the source of the noise, Chronol threw another stone in the same direction.

"Who goes there?" one of them called out. He immediately threw a third, much harder this time. The two guards quickly drew their weapons and closed in on the commotion. Soon as they stepped away from the gate Chronol snuck in behind them and entered the city unnoticed. He darted into the shadows between buildings, peeking through windows to check for soldiers that might be inside. Finding an empty home, he stealthily entered and searched for a change of clothes. Furniture was overturned and thrown around the house, splatters of red streaked across the wall and a faint smell of blood still lingered in the air. Unfortunately, the place had clearly been ransacked and only a few women's garments remained. He sighed for a moment, then noticed a glimmer in the corner. Walking over, he found it was a small, silver mirror. Looking into his reflection, he gasped. His black, spiked hair was dirty, as was his face. Bits of dirt and sand could be seen in his goatee. He stared into the polished metal, bringing it closer and closer to his face. To his shock, glowing green eyes stared back at him where brown eyes once were. He blinked over and over, closing one eye and then the other, trying to make sure the reflection was real. "What… what happened to my eyes??" The more anxious he got, the brighter they glowed. He closed his eyes and took a moment to collect himself, trying to calm down. Eventually the glow dimmed back to how it was when he first looked into the mirror. "There's no time for this now… I need to find some clothes and get out of here before I'm found. I will deal with you later," he thought, pointing at his reflection. Pocketing the mirror he continued his search, going from home to home, finding each of them either burned, occupied or raided. Taverns, smithies, tailors, the school; almost everything was destroyed or burned in some way.

After searching several places, he finally came across another burned home and found a sack in the wreckage that was pinned under some debris. He carefully lifted the rubble, trying not to cause a cave in or make noise, using his foot to slide the bag out behind him. Inside there were two outfits, a dagger, and a small steel emblem. He gripped the symbol in his palm and closed his eyes for a moment. This crest was worn by the city guards of Thoros, an identical one hung from Chronol's belt. He turned it over and looked at the back. Etched into the metal was the name Bohrien. "He was a good man…" he whispered, putting the emblem in his pocket and everything else back in the sack. Staying hidden, he snuck back to the part of the wall that he scaled when he escaped the first time. Following the same method, he kicked off the wall and landed on the same building as before. As he set foot on the roof, he looked up to see his city ablaze. The smell of smoke filled the air while shouts and screams of combat could be heard in the distance. Startled, Chronol took an instinctual step back. His foot slipped off the roof and he began to fall. His fingertips gripped the edge at the last second, keeping him from plummeting to the ground. His eyes wide, he shook his head, trying to clear his focus. He pulled himself back up and looked at the city again. No blazing buildings, no shouting, only darkness dotted by scattered torches and bonfires. Chronol rubbed his eyes, taking a deep breath and looked once more at his home. It remained dark and peaceful, only crickets and murmuring in the background. After regaining his composure, he continued his escape, leaping to the wall then down to the ground and running into the woods.

Once he was a safe distance from town, he took a moment to get changed, placing Maksis near him on the ground. He decided to bury his armor just in case any patrols came through the area. Looking at it one last time, shrouded in darkness with only bits of moonlight slipping through the leafy canopy above, he felt the hole in the armor once more. Rubbing his chest, there was only smooth skin under his fingertips, no cut or wound of any kind. "How did that happen?" he wondered. "Well, I hate to leave you behind, but I can't be seen wearing you right now." With a final glance he covered the armor with dirt and some bits of foliage to hide the disturbed earth. Tiny paws began trying to dig it up but were stopped by Chronol's hand. "No, Maks. That needs to stay here. Leave it, boy."

He collected a set of ten small stones before digging a small hole. Placing Bohrien's guard emblem into it, he closed his eyes and spent a moment in silence surrounded by the chirps of frogs and crickets. "Rest in peace my friend, I'll see you on the other side." He gently covered the hole with dirt and placed the stones around it in a circle. Reaching back into the bag he pulled the dagger out and held it reverently in front of the circle with his head bowed. "With your permission, I use this in your honor, brother." He took the dagger and hooked it into the back of his belt.

Chronol began walking south towards Eppildor, taking his time. His furry little companion hopped through the grass alongside him. It wasn't long before he felt the need for rest and took to the branches as usual, carrying Maksis up with him in a pouch on his hip. When they found a comfortable spot to sleep, he reclined and laid the pup on his chest, gently petting him for a bit. The small wolfhound licked his master's chin and laid flat on his chest. The soldier pulled the small mirror from his pocket again, staring into the green glow that stared back at him. "Can this be real? What sort of magic would have caused this? Will my eyes ever be normal again? How did this happen? When did this happen? Have they been like this since the battle?" These thoughts swirled through his mind, question after question, with no answers in sight. "I can't have people looking at me like this, I'm going to draw attention. Thankfully there was a cloak in that bag. Looks like I'll be keeping the hood up to hide my eyes as much as possible." Maksis turned around curiously and spotted the mirror. He crawled up to the shiny metal and looked at himself. The pup pawed at his reflection, wagging his tail gently. "See something you like in there, little one?" Chronol smiled, gently playing with the swaying tail before him. Maksis spun around and pounced on his master's hand, wrestling and playing with him. The two tussled for a few minutes, the pup occasionally looking back at his reflection, expecting the other wolfhound to join in the game. They continued playing until Maks grew tired. The hound snuggled up in a ball near his master's neck, Chronol blanketing the small creature with his hand. He closed his eyes and drifted to sleep, thinking of the next day's journey, and the chance of finding survivors in Eppildor.

3

The Tracker

Piercing through the chaos of battle was the sound of a child crying. "What're you doing out here? You need to get inside NOW!" the soldier cried out. The child looked at him, tears streaming from his eyes. The boy screamed but no sound came out. Chronol's eyes grew wide; reaching out, time seemed to slow down as a cold, iron ballista bolt crept through the air, growing closer to the boy. Blood sprayed forth, misting the air like a red fog. The bolt dripped crimson from the tip, the child's scream echoing from the distance, growing louder and louder.

Chronol opened his eyes and stared into the leaves in front of him. "Please no," he thought as tears filled his eyes. "I don't want to remember any more… make it stop…. please…." He closed his eyes but was immediately confronted with Daran's face once again. "I'm sorry… I'm so… so sorry. Please forgive me… I wanted to protect you… I wanted to protect all of you…" One after another, the faces of his slain friends flashed through his mind, all of them now lying lifeless in a pit outside of Thoros. "I couldn't save any of you… I'm useless… 'Protector of Thoros'... I couldn't save any of you..." He pulled Bohrien's dagger from its sheath and stared at his reflection in the blade, a green glow emanating from it. The craftsmanship of Thoron steel is unlike anything else in existence. This dagger was used every day, but still remained polished and shining like a trophy meant to be displayed on a mantle. As his mind continued to torment him with face after face, he was reminded of Kaerill. "She still needs me. Her and anyone else that survived. I can still protect them." He shook his head and wiped his tears, putting the blade away.

21

"Come along, little one. It's time to get moving," he whispered to the sleeping pup, scratching his ears till Maksis woke up.

The two set out on their journey to Eppildor. They made their way south, staying to the woods and avoiding any roaming patrols along the way. After almost two days of travel they found themselves at the outskirts of the town. It was small and quaint, with little farms scattered throughout. Everything seemed fine at first glance, no ruckus or destruction, no signs of battle, no displays of gore and conquest. It was eerie to see such a calm-looking town, knowing the genocide that had happened just a couple day's walk to the north. Chronol remained skeptical and concerned, all his senses on high alert. He scanned the perimeter of the city but found only the usual number of guards in place. Nevertheless, he kept to the outskirts and made his way to higher ground west of the city. From this vantage point, he could see the majority of the small town and was able to observe everyone's behavior. He watched people go about their business, seemingly unaware of the bloody slaughter that took place just a few days earlier. Merchants selling their goods, people shopping, craftsmen making their wares, children playing; everything looked normal. "It's like nothing even happened…" he whispered, feeling a sense of unease and shock. "My people almost completely wiped from the face of the earth, and here people buy apples and laugh as if everything is right in the world." He watched carefully, making a mental note of where and how often the guards patrolled. At the same time, he checked the movements of the villagers, seeing if anyone acted suspicious, keeping to the shadows, avoiding guards or minimizing eye contact. Unfortunately, no one stood out to him as a possible Thoron in hiding. Chronol looked to see if he recognized anyone but at this distance it was impossible to tell. "I guess we're going in there, boy. You need to stay hidden and quiet," he explained to his pup, patting his head. Using his dagger, he poked a few holes in the front of his bag, then tucked Maksis inside. Lifting the bag to inspect his work, little brown and silver eyes peered through the holes, the bottom of the bag wiggling as Maks tried to wag his tail. "That should work. Good boy," Chronol smiled, looking into the hound's eyes.

Adjusting his hood to make sure his cloak obscured his eyes, he took his hidden pup and headed towards the west entrance to town. Being a smaller town, it didn't really have much in terms of walls or fencing around the perimeter, so it was easy to find a way in that avoided the patrolling guards. Walking towards the market area, he casually glanced around, checking people's faces while trying not to draw attention to himself. Even up close no one appeared familiar to him. Getting deeper into the town, the smell of meat cooking from one of the merchant stalls enveloped him. His stomach grumbled a little as he breathed in the enticing aroma, realizing it had been over a week since his last properly cooked and seasoned meal. His only nourishment came from the different woodland creatures he would hunt and roast over a fire for Maksis and himself. This smell was so smokey and tantalizing he could almost taste it. Reaching into a small pouch, he felt a few coins rustling around inside. "Who knows when I'll get another chance, maybe I should take advantage while I can," he thought, looking towards the source of the aroma. A merchant was seasoning some skewered cuts of beef grilling over a fire. After purchasing a skewer, he walked to a side ally to pull back his hood a little while staying out of sight. Bringing the meat up to his nose, he took a deep breath, taking in the scents of the delicious gift that beckoned him. But when he went to take a bite, a soft whimpering sound coming from his hip stopped him. "Really?" he whispered, looking down at his pouch. "Alright, just one." Opening the top of the pouch, he smiled when Maksis popped his head out and stared at the steaming treat. Chronol carefully pulled a cube to the edge of the skewer then fed it to his furry companion. His tiny teeth gobbled it up enthusiastically and in no time the piece was devoured. "That's enough, back in you go before you're spotted." He tucked Maks back into the pouch, closing it once again, then ate the rest of the meat, savoring every juicy bite. Despite staying fed during his travels, that meal made him feel like it was the first he'd had in a week. Once it was finished, he pulled his hood forward again and sat down in the alley against a building. Chronol sighed and closed his eyes for a moment, letting his food settle. For the briefest moment he forgot about the world around him, the soldiers pursuing him, the destruction of his town. For just a few seconds everything drifted away.

"Don't stare, Alda. Come on," someone said nearby. He looked towards the sound and noticed a woman holding a child by the hand. The child had been looking at him sitting against the wall and was being ushered down the street. Reality came flooding back in, his senses back on high alert as he picked himself up and walked through the alley away from the family that had noticed him. He continued making his way through town, doing his best to avoid the paths of the patrolling guards, but despite his best efforts he failed to find any familiar faces. After checking most of the town he found a small tavern and decided to go inside. The tavern was very simple and quiet, with just a handful of customers. Two men sat near the bar, one with a flute, the other with a guitar, playing a soft melody while people purchased their drinks. There were two couples sitting together at a table in the center of the tavern, drinking wine and eating some food the barkeep had just brought out to them. Another pair of gentlemen sat off to the side, keeping to the shadows of the room. Chronol went to the barkeep and purchased a glass of water, taking a seat at an empty table adjacent to a few other patrons. He listened in on the conversations around him, hoping to get some useful information.

"Jordah needs to just accept that there's not much harvest this season," one of the ladies said. "It isn't as if you did something different to grow less crops. It's just been a bit colder than usual. It happens."

"I wish it was that simple," one of the men responded. "He's been very aggressive lately about making sure we have enough crops to supply the Kohtans with their taxes. I do understand his position, though. They don't care if the crops are less fruitful this year, they still expect the same offering and that will mean less he can sell to take care of his family and workers. We're all affected by it if the crops don't produce."

"Those cursed Kohtans," the other gentleman growled. "All they do is take, take, take."

"Keep your voice down!" his wife pleaded.

"I'll speak my mind, woman," he argued. "I'm not going to sit and cower in my own hometown. They came here, took over, and expect us to pay them for the privilege of still having breath. They took all our best fighters and left us with these barely competent soldiers. They come and take whatever they please and expect the town to continue to produce what they need regardless of how the seasons change from year to year. Just because we've accepted the situation doesn't make it any better."

"Well, Diasin, it's not like we have an alternative," the other man responded. "What are we going to do? Stop giving them what they ask and get everyone killed? Give up our lives over some grain? We have no army to fight them. We have no way of escape. We have no choice but to accept our lot in life and be thankful that they at least let us live here in relative peace."

"What about the Caldorians?" the man's wife asked. "Do you think they'll ever make it this far into the empire?"

"The Caldorians don't seek conquest," her husband explained. "The Wars of the Two Kingdoms only keep happening because these greedy Kohtans keep trying to expand into the Kingdom of Caldor's territory. They'll never come here, they're content to defend their borders and stay in their own lands."

"It would be amazing if that happened, though," she smiled. "I hear the Caldorians behave almost completely opposite of the Kohtans. When they find a new town and want to bring it into their kingdom, they actually bring gifts of food and resources, offering protection under their banner. They leave highly skilled knights in every town that accepts them and makes sure they're properly looked after and taken care of. It sounds like paradise."

"No place is perfect," Diasin chimed in, "but it certainly would be better than here." Their conversation was interrupted by the sound of the tavern doors opening. Four Kohtan guards entered, laughing and carrying on as they made their way to the bar. "Speak of the devils themselves…" he grumbled. His wife gently elbowed him in the side to silence him. The Kohtans ordered their drinks and continued their banter while they waited to be served. "So pleased with themselves when they didn't even take part in the battle." Chronol's eyes widened upon hearing the man's muttered comment.

"More like the massacre," said the other man. "Those Thorons didn't stand a chance with the outrageous forces the Kohtans sent."

"Can you blame them?" asked Diasin. "Thoros was the last great threat to the Kohtan empire on this side of the border. If the Thorons ever decided to expand their territory, the Kohtans would have been on the losing side of the battle until they could amass all their forces in one place. Coming in with everything they had was the only way to guarantee victory."

"Everyone knows the Thorons never cared about conquest and expansion," his wife added. "There must have been some other reason for the attack. Those poor people… wiped from the face of the earth. The only survivors conscripted into the empire's army, as always."

"Actually," the other woman corrected, "I heard they left no survivors. No one was conscripted. It's the first city they've taken over where they left no one alive."

"Really?" she asked.

"I don't blame them," Diasin sighed. "Who in their right mind would leave any survivors in Thoros knowing what they're capable of? Even a handful of them would be a problem for the empire if they grouped together and trained others. They would find no shortage of allies wanting to overthrow the oppression of the Kohtans." He was elbowed yet again by his wife as the guards made their way to an adjacent table and took a seat. Chronol sat there, staring into his glass, their words echoing in his head.

"I can't wait for the new supplies to come in," one of the soldiers smiled. "Just think of the new weapons we'll get once they start mining all that Thoron steel. We're going to be unstoppable."

"Yes, I have to agree," another nodded. "Killing them and taking the Mines of Sharef for ourselves was by far a better solution than bartering trade with them. No worrying about competition having the same quality steel, no need to stress over trade agreements and managing cost. Just kill them all and take the mines, simple and efficient." Before the soldier could continue, a glass shattered at the table next to them. Chronol's hand trembled, blood dripping from the glass shards in his hand. He placed a coin on the table for the damage and walked to the door. "Hey, you there! Where are you going?" the soldier called out. Chronol left the tavern, closing the door behind him. The soldier ran to the door, his allies following closely behind. He stepped out and looked around, but the stranger was nowhere to be found. "Split up and search for him, he can't have gone far." They searched all over but found no trace of him. He had completely disappeared, leaving nothing behind except some blood and broken glass where he'd sat.

"The mines…?" Chronol asked, staring at a tree outside of town. "They killed everyone... everyone I knew and loved... over the mines?" The green glow in his eyes flared and swirled as his rage grew. "We would've traded with them! These bloodthirsty animals would rather kill off an entire population instead of opening up trade with us?" He punched the tree, splintering the wood beneath his knuckles. His breathing was heavy from trying to contain his emotions and his body trembled with anger. "Everyone is dead over some stupid iron?" he shouted, punching the tree again. "I lost everything! Everyone! They're all dead so these monsters could make some new swords!" With every word he punched the tree, again and again, grunting and growling, swinging with increasing ferocity, faster and harder. The more he raged, the more bloodstained and broken the tree became until, finally he stopped and fell to his knees, panting. All of the faces in the mass grave flashed through his mind yet again. He closed his eyes, his teeth gnashing together as his fists trembled. The soldier cried out in pain, not from his injured hands but from the realization, from the fact that his entire civilization was lost over greed. Chronol shouted to the heavens, his roar echoing through the forest like an enraged dragon.

He knelt there for a moment catching his breath. Looking down at his palms, he began picking the glass and wood from his hands. When his wounds were cleaned out he stood up and started aimlessly wandering east. His feet almost dragged across the ground with every step. After a couple miles he stopped and laid on the ground, curling up in a ball. He began weeping, wondering what reason there was to continue moving forward. His crying was interrupted by a small tongue licking his head. The soldier opened his eyes to find Maksis staring at him, wagging his little tail as he whined and pawed at his master. Chronol reached out and pet him, pulling him in close and holding the pup against his chest. There was no sign of his people in Eppildor, but based on the conversation he overheard, it was safe to assume any survivors were killed if they came to town, unaware it was dangerous to reveal themselves as Thorons. With no other lead and unsure of what to do next, he lay there staring into the brush, tears still dripping from his eyes until they could no longer stay open. As the adrenaline wore off and sleep took him, his only solace was the little life clutched tightly in his arms.

Chapter 4

The Determined

"I can't give up on my people…" Chronol whispered to himself, the sun creeping over the horizon. "I have to keep searching. If anyone survived, I need to be there for them… help them survive… protect them. Where could they be? Where would they go if not Eppildor?" He stared at the grass, slowly petting his wolfhound while losing himself in thought, imagining about the different ways to escape the city and the directions people could have gone. "East?" he thought to himself. "No, the army was East. Anyone headed that way would have been slaughtered. West? I suppose some could have hid inside the mines, but they'd be trapped and it would only be a matter of time before they were discovered." He sat up and rested his back against a tree, still staring into the bed of green he had just been laying on. "North would take them towards Atera. A larger city… more friendly with The Empire… not a safe option. Anyone who might've escaped there would probably have been turned in to the Kohtans and slain. Chances of survival are slim… South was a dead end as well… Where? They said 'Thorons', there must be more than just me alive out here. Where would they have sought refuge…?" He pondered more and more, mapping out different routes in his head, thinking of every possible alternative. While going over the ways south toward Eppildor, he was reminded of a side road that went southeast. Anyone taking this route could have avoided running into the invading army, especially if it was during the chaos. "Servil… Servil is down that path if you go far enough. It's not as close as Eppildor, but it's small, out of the way, and not particularly friendly with The Empire. Perhaps some of my people escaped there and hid amongst the villagers." When he thought this out loud, a pair of little silver and brown eyes looked up at him from his lap. "What do you think, Maks? That seems like the next place to search." The tiny ball of fur yawned widely, stretching its small arms and paws forward. Maks stood up in his lap and shook off the remaining grogginess. Then he hopped down into the grass, wagged his tail, looked back at his master and let out a small bark. "Alright then," Chronol smiled, "I guess we're headed for Servil." He picked up his belongings and headed southeast, holding out hope of finding more survivors.

They made their way through the woods, stopping and hiding to observe travelers from a distance whenever hearing others approach. Each time they hid, there was always that moment of tension, waiting to see who would come walking by. Would it be a patrol of soldiers? A merchant peddling their goods from town to town? A family traveling home? Thankfully, most of the trip was rather uneventful, running into mostly civilians and other non-threats. However, when the sun began to drift behind the horizon, he heard a different sound ahead of him.

"Please, don't! I beg of you!" a woman's voice shouted. Hearing this he rushed forward to the edge of the treeline. In the path up ahead were three bandits clad in black. Their mouths were covered with red sashes, their skin tanned and darkened from years on the road. Their swords, sharp but worn, were clearly used frequently. In the center of the men was a woman and her child. She was young, her brown hair pulled up and pinned in place, with a lighter tan than her captors. The woman was trying to pull her small son behind her to hide him under the large bag full of various goods that adorned her back. His little blue eyes peeked around his mother's dress, his trembling hands gripping her skirt as he stared at the men threatening them. "Please, just leave us be!" she pleaded. "We have no quarrel with you, we're just trying to make a living to survive!" One of the bandits laughed quietly, approaching the woman. Chronol noticed an emblem on the man's bag. It was one he'd seen quite recently, in black and gold, hanging between the bodies of his fallen comrades. In a flash, the memories of all his loved ones appeared before him, their bloodied faces lying piled on top of each other. His gaze grew wide and the green in his eyes flared like emerald flames.

The bandit reached towards the woman's face, but just before he could grab her, a pristine blade whistled through the air and impaled the man's palm, pinning it to the tree behind him. He yelled out in pain, his allies turning to look in the direction the blade came from. They saw an enraged swordsman jumping through the air towards them.

"Who's this now?" One bandit shouted, trying to raise his sword to block the incoming attack, but to no avail. His attacker's blade severed off his hand and continued forward, embedding itself halfway through his torso, killing him almost instantly. Chronol immediately pulled his sword from the corpse and turned to his next terrified target.

"Hey, back off!" the bandit shouted as he quickly stepped back, hurling a small throwing knife into Chronol's shoulder, before thrusting his sword out in front of him. The swordsman's pace was unaffected as he continued to charge forward, his bare hand grabbing the man's sword by the blade and moving it out of the way before cutting him down, leaving him bleeding and motionless on the forest floor. Finally, he turned to the one pinned to the tree. The thief stared wide-eyed in horror at having just seen his friends slain in an instant.

"W-w...wait... now just hold on a second... This... this was... it's just..." He fumbled for words, trying to find something to say to spare himself from the same fate, but before any kind of plea could be uttered, Chronol reeled back with his sword and brought it down on the bandit. Over and over, he chopped like a furious butcher, swinging faster and harder. Letting out a guttural yell, he took the sword with both hands and continued hacking away until all that remained was a pile of meat and bones.

The soldier breathed heavily, staring at the pile, swinging one final time, splattering more red across his already blood-sprayed clothing. He turned and glared at the second bandit he had killed, the body lying motionless in a red pool. Chronol looked towards the mother and her child and suddenly froze in place. His breathing stopped, seeing the dread and fear in their eyes. They stared at the bestial, blood-soaked figure that intervened. It was clear from the looks on their faces that they were unsure if they had been saved, or if they were about to be killed by something more vicious than the bandits that originally threatened their lives. As he calmed down, the glow in his eyes dimmed. "It's alright," he gently assured them. "I'm not going to hurt you." He slowly laid his sword on the floor, trying to calm the family, but the woman still stepped back, keeping her son tucked away behind her. "Are you hurt? Is your child injured in any way?" The woman remained silent, just staring and quickly shook her head. "I'm sorry for what you've seen," he apologized, looking down at the gory mess surrounding them. Finally feeling the blade in his shoulder, he reached up and pulled it out, throwing it to the ground before covering the wound with his hand. He looked back down at the corpses, thinking for a moment. Kneeling down beside the two farthest from the family, he took their coin and tucked it away in his pouch. Chronol left the third body alone, not wanting to approach the already terrified family. "I'll be on my way, you're free to go. Safety be with you." He bid them farewell and slowly collected his sword and dagger before walking towards the trees ahead.

"Wh… who are you?" the woman quietly asked. The soldier paused and thought for a moment, considering the possible repercussions of revealing his identity.

"I'm no one…" he answered, then started walking away once more.

"Thank you, Sir no one!" a small voice called out. He paused again for a moment before disappearing into the woods, his small, furry companion bounding behind him.

Treking deeper into the woods, the look on the woman's face stuck in his mind. No one had ever looked at him that way before. Having spent years guarding the city, being a protector for his fellow Thorons, he was used to being looked at a certain way. Everyone showed him respect and gratitude in Thoros; in turn, he was dedicated and kind. He would have done anything for his people, and they'd known that. It showed in the way the city had treated him. The only time he'd ever been looked at with fear was in the face of an enemy, but even then he kept his composure, giving quarter to any who would surrender. Losing control like he just had was something Chronol was not familiar with, and it scared him. It was one thing to terrify an enemy, but for the ones he was saving to be just as scared of him… this was a side of himself he'd never seen before.

His thoughts were interrupted by a trickling sound not far from where he was walking. Following the bubbling noise, he found a small creek. It flowed through the woods, carving a path between the trees and intersecting with the trail Chronol was on. An occasional fish, too small to eat, could be seen swimming along with the gentle current. Looking down at the mess his clothes were in, he decided to try and get cleaned up as best he could. At the water's edge, his view into the creek was interrupted by his reflection looking back at him. The soldier stared at himself, confronted by what the boy and his mother had seen. Glimmering green eyes, surrounded by a face painted crimson red, stared back at him. His appearance startled him for a moment. He'd seen combat before, but never had anything left him in such a bloody state. "I look like… a monster…" he thought to himself. While still staring at his reflection, Maksis hopped playfully into the water. Chronol watched his face distort in the ripples, the glowing green eyes still looking back at him. Turning away, unable to bear the sight any longer, he removed his clothes and weapons, setting them on the edge of the water, before easing himself into the creek. The water was quickly tinted red as he began washing the blood spatter from his skin. While working to remove the stains, his thoughts returned to what had just happened. As if seeing it from a third-person view, the events replayed in his head. He saw himself brutalize those thieves, saw the loss of control at the sight of the Kohtan markings on their gear, saw the terror his actions invoked in the very people he wanted to protect. The red tint slowly drifted downstream until there was nothing left on him to wash away. After cleaning himself up, he opened the bag from Thoros. He cleaned and wrapped the gashes in his hand and shoulder then changed into the other set of clothing, burying the bloody garments he'd removed. Seeing his wolfhound still enjoying the water, he sat for a moment and cleaned his blades, making sure they were properly taken care of before sheathing them. When Maksis finished paddling around in the water he crawled out, shaking his fur dry. Looking at his reflection once more, Chronol saw a familiar face. His eyes still glowed but the rest remained as he remembered. "I'm still… me… right?" he pondered. Trying to clear his mind, he shook his head and continued through the woods.

The now cleaned soldier traveled through the forest, watching out for any signs of life, including any tracks that might have come from other Thorons making their way towards Servil. He unfortunately found no signs of other survivors, only a couple small woodland creatures he was able to cook for food. Nevertheless, he kept heading towards Servil until he heard a group of people coming toward him from up ahead. Chronol quickly scooped up his companion and scaled a tree, hiding in the branches, waiting and watching for movement. It wasn't long before a handful of Kohtan soldiers came into view. They settled a little ways down from him, just barely within earshot.

"I'm exhausted…" one of the patrol groaned, sitting down before flopping onto his back, a piece of ration in his hand.

"Yeah, well don't let the Commander hear you say that," another soldier replied. "He's having no complaints from anyone today. Something's put him in a foul mood."

"More than usual…" the first soldier said quietly, chewing his food. "What's the point of this search anyways? So what if a Thoron or two survive? What can they do that their entire people couldn't? There's no stopping the Empire. It's a hungry beast with no end to it's appetite for conquest."

"It's a pointless endeavor," another soldier agreed, "but there's nothing we can do. The Overlord insists on it, and so it must be done."

"I think it makes him look weak and desperate," the lounging soldier murmured. "Worrying so much over one or two survivors that probably don't even exist. I mean, really… wha…" His sentence was cut short as a larger soldier interrupted, resting his boot on the lying soldier's throat.

"No one speaks of the Overlord in such a way," he snarled, "and to do so is treason." The first soldier struggled, patting the side of his Commander's leg. His pleas were of no use, as the boot remained until his eyes drifted closed and his skin turned blue. "Does anyone else have any comments they'd like to make regarding our leader or our mission?" the Commander asked, glaring at his soldiers. They all averted their eyes, not saying a word. "Good…" He walked back to his corner, sitting against a tree as an awkward silence enveloped the group.

"Monster… killing his own soldier over an innocent comment. Apparently, they're still on the lookout for survivors and anyone who might be harboring them," he thought to himself. "It was probably for the best that I didn't reveal my identity to that family. I'd better stay anonymous from here on out to protect those around me." He stayed put waiting for them to leave, but when the sun began to set, they decided to make camp. Once it was clear that there would be no moving on tonight, Chronol got comfortable, planning to keep an eye on the camp throughout the night. The soldier in him thought for a moment of ambushing them in the darkness, but as soon as the thought crossed his mind, he remembered his lost control earlier that day and decided to keep his distance and just wait for them to pack up and leave.

The night seemed longer than usual. With the moonlight mostly blocked by the canopy of trees, the only real light in the area was the glow of the campfire. The soft crackling of flame in the distance mixed with the rustling leaves and chirping crickets. The smell of burning wood surrounded him as he watched them intently, unable to let himself sleep for fear of discovery. Hour after hour they slept in shifts, two always keeping watch while the other six slept. He measured them, ascertaining whatever he could from watching their interactions: who was in charge, who was the lowest rank, which ones seemed more fit and battle ready, and which seemed weaker. He took in as much as he could, ready to use that information in a fight, should the need arise. However, when the sun rose, they woke and ate before smothering the flames and moving on, walking right under him as they continued their search. They never even bothered to bury their dead comrade, just took his coin and left his body in the brush. With the immediate threat avoided, he climbed out of the tree and headed southeast, hoping their presence now behind him meant the way forward was clear of further patrols.

After a few more hours of traveling, he had finally located what he was looking for. Approaching the outskirts, he found himself looking at the small village of Servil. Similar in size to Eppildor, though a little smaller, it had more farms and mills than its western counterpart due to its main export being grain. Not familiar with this town, Chronol spent the better part of the day keeping to the treeline, circling the perimeter of the town, trying to get a better idea of where to enter and survey things. Having a much flatter landscape than Eppildor meant he wouldn't be able to stay on the outskirts and observe this town like the previous one. He would need to find a better vantage point. During his reconnaissance he came across a farm with an exceptionally tall mill on the property. It was close enough to the outskirts that he felt confident he could get to it without being seen, especially under the cloak of darkness. If he could get to the top, he'd have a clear view of the town and its inhabitants and could figure out his plan of action from there. With this goal in mind, he stayed in the trees near the farm and watched the farmers work, learning their numbers, their routines, and figuring out which route would give him the least chance of being spotted.

Chronol continued his watch until nightfall, then made his approach under the cover of darkness. Creeping carefully through the farm, he kept low to avoid the windows of the home which faced the mill. It had been an hour or so since the lights in the house had been put out, but he remained cautious nonetheless. Slipping over the fencing, he made his way to the mill, keeping an eye on the adjacent farmhouse, watching for any movement. When he reached the door to the mill, it was locked. A broken lock would alert the farmers to his presence in the morning, so he searched around the back for a way up. His only option was to use the edges of the uneven stones in the walls as small finger and footholds to try scaling the outside of the building. Slowly climbing up the side of the building, he carefully made sure each grip was as secure as possible before reaching for another stone. Slipping more than once, the climb was treacherous, leaving him to rely on his finger strength to keep from plummeting back to the ground. After several minutes and a few close calls, he reached the top. Chronol perched himself on the roof and pried a couple boards loose so he could enter, replacing them as best he could once inside. Finally in a safe position at the top of the mill, he found a place to lie down and rest for a few hours before sunrise. "When the sun rises and the town is awake, I'll be able to observe and hopefully spot some survivors in hiding." Chronol dozed off with these thoughts, wondering if the morning would finally bring him closer to what's left of his people.

5

The Traitor

Bits of sunlight crept through the roof of the mill, coaxing the soldier's eyes open as the sounds of farm workers echoed around him. He slowly awoke from his sleep, still somewhat groggy, and tried to focus his eyes. Chronol felt his chest but found nothing. His eyes quickly grew wide as he looked around him, realizing his wolfhound was nowhere in sight. "Maks…" he whispered softly, "where are you? …Maks!" He scanned the area around him looking for any signs of his companion, when he suddenly saw some movement in the pile of grain beside him. Tiny, familiar eyes peeked out at him. Chronol let out a sigh of relief at the sight of them. "There you are… What are you doing in there? Come," he called out. The little creature crawled out, carrying a small twig in his mouth. He placed it in front of his master then sat in front of it, wagging his tail. "Really? That's what you were looking for?" he smiled. "Very well…" Picking it up, he instructed the pup to stay while preparing to toss the twig. He gently threw it to the other side of the space they were in. The pup looked back at it as it landed. "Eh eh eh… stayyy…" Maksis faced forward and stared at his master, his tail lying still. "Good boy… go get em!" The wolfhound darted for the stick, grabbing it and wrestling it down like he had captured an animal. "Cease!" Chronol called out, watching the hound stop at the sound of the command. "Bring it here," he instructed. The pup quickly collected the stick and brought it back, placing it in front of him and sitting down, awaiting the next instruction. "That's my boy," he smiled, petting the little ball of fur as it wrestled with his hand. They played and trained like this for some time while the sun continued to rise.

When they finished, Chronol stood up and lifted the loosened piece of roof from the night before and peeked out towards Servil. Surveying everyone in town and hoping for a spark of recognition, he kept his eyes peeled for anyone acting strangely; avoiding being seen, sneaking through the shadows, anything that could indicate they were on the run. He watched all morning, hoping this town wouldn't be a dead end like the last one. After about an hour, he noticed a cloaked individual that seemed to walk normally through the town, but in the most inefficient way possible. Chronol realized, as he continued to watch the person, that all the paths they seemed to bypass or avoid were ones that had guards posted. "Could it be...? Have I finally found someone?" Holding on to the hope in that thought, he continued to watch the individual making their way through town. At one point they stopped at a merchant stall, apparently looking to buy something, but in reality, it appeared they were avoiding a pair of guards that were heading down that street. Everything in their movements indicated they didn't want to be spotted by the Kohtans. "They must be hiding from the army... either this is a criminal or one of my people... I have to find out for sure..." Chronol's eyes followed the mysterious figure until they eventually made their way into a tavern on the east side of the village. At that moment, a bell began to ring from the nearby farmhouse, and the workers started making their way into the building for lunch. Deciding that this was his best chance to get to the individual before they left the tavern and potentially disappeared, he quickly climbed down from the mill and darted into town. The sun shone brightly overhead, leaving him less shadows to hide in than the person he had watched earlier. The breeze carried the smell of fresh grain through the town, mixing with the various foods being sold on the street. Chronol traveled through the streets, trying to use the same pattern the cloaked figure used to avoid the posted guards. Carefully, he made his way through town, trying to blend in with the villagers until eventually reaching the tavern. Placing his hand on the door, his heart began to race. The thought that this door was the last thing standing between him and another possible survivor made him tremble with anticipation for a moment. Slowly, he opened the door and peered into the dimly lit tavern. There were a few patrons sitting scattered about the room, each at their own small table. Chronol approached the portly, young bartender who stood cleaning the counter and purchased a glass of water from him. Drink in hand, he started walking around, inspecting the patrons under the guise of deciding where to sit. Making his way through the room, he noticed the cloaked figure he'd been tracking, sitting alone in a darker part of the tavern eating his meal. Chronol sat at a table in front of the stranger, taking a drink of water and setting down his glass.

"Kaaldoth's strength be with you," he said quietly to the cloaked figure. The man gasped, instantly looked up to see who had spoken. Tanned skin and dark hair were revealed under the man's hood and looking into the terrified blue eyes staring at him, it was immediately clear to Chronol that this was not a Thoron. Upon further inspection, he noticed the Kohtan military insignia branded into the man's neck. His eyes glowed with rage, but his initial shock and anger was quickly calmed by the face of the man in front of him. This wasn't the face of a fighter or a guard, but of someone scared and on the run. The man tried to hurry up and walk away but Chronol stomped his foot on top of the stranger's, pinning it down with such force that the man couldn't escape. He winced in pain, trying to keep quiet and not make a scene. With a quick look around to see if anyone had noticed, he quietly sat back down.

"Please sir," he pleaded softly, "I wish for no trouble. I was just eating and would like to be on my way."

"I think not," Chronol replied, pressing down hard on the man's foot, watching his eyes squint in pain. "You'll not be going anywhere until you answer some questions. Let's start with why you're sneaking around town. Are you some sort of criminal?"

"Something like that…" the man replied looking down at the table. "Let's just say it's best for me not to be noticed by the Kohtan soldiers."

"Explain," the Thoron demanded, "best not to be vague when your life hangs in the balance. Why hide from the Kohtans? You have their military brand on your neck, are you not a soldier yourself?"

"Somewhat…" the man replied. "My name is Vaelin, I'm a Weaver from Grensweld."

"A Weaver?" Chronol asked, "are you one of those people that can heal wounds with your magic?"

"Yes," he nodded, "our kind are born with the innate ability to channel our powers into mending wounds and bringing people back to good health."

"So how does that lead to you being branded by the military?" Chronol wondered. "And why are you hiding from them?"

"Well, I'm not sure how familiar you are with the military tactics of the Kohtans," Vaelin explained, "but they are ruthless. They storm their target with the full might of their army and rain hell upon them until they surrender. Once they've secured a victory, they go through and find any useful survivors and conscript them into their army. They brand you," he explained, showing the mark on his neck, "and you belong to their military force until you die, whether you like it or not. This is how they maintain and grow their forces from one invasion to the next. They take all the soldiers and healers and magic users from each province they conquer and add them to their ranks. I was one such conscript. As to why I'm hiding from them, I'm a deserter. I was…" he hesitated to continue, having trouble looking Chronol in the eyes. "I… was part of the Battle of Thoros…"

Chronol's eyes glowed bright hearing these words. He fought to maintain his composure knowing he now sat face to face with one of the opposing forces that destroyed his home and his people. "So, this is why you tried to run from me… You recognized the traditional greeting of the Thorons."

"Yes…" the man admitted, his voice shaky. "I thought you had all perished. When you spoke, I feared I sat before a ghost. Looking up and seeing that unnatural green glow in your eyes, it was as if my fears had been made real. I simply wanted to escape the specter haunting me from my past mistakes, but you turned out to be flesh and blood as you stopped my escape."

Hearing this, Chronol pulled his hood down slightly, attempting to obscure the glow coming from his eyes. "Continue," he whispered.

"I am so sorry," Vaelin apologized, "I wanted nothing to do with that massacre. I was forced to come along and make sure their soldiers remained fit for battle. Their forces were terrifying, an ocean of soldiers marching on the city like a blanket of darkness, their steps shook the ground like thunder. They had monstrous machines of war launching every manner of destructive force through the sky, destroying walls and buildings. When the dragons came to defend the city I thought we were done for, but their Shadowmages turned the very skies to the will of the Kohtans, conjuring fire and lightning, striking the beasts as they flew."

"So that's how Kaaldoth fell…" Chronol sighed, looking down in remembrance. "What happened next?"

"Well," he continued, "once the gates had fallen I was dispatched with a unit of soldiers to raid the city. I was just supposed to be there to heal any soldier who got injured. I expected to see an extraordinary fight, but when we entered the city we found soldiers and civilians pinned under the various rubble that had fallen from the buildings. My unit marched through, killing them all one by one. The horror of what I witnessed will live on in my mind for the rest of my life. Men, women, and children who were being crushed and posed no threat to anyone anymore, were stabbed and sliced apart like cattle. I couldn't bring myself to watch. I tried to avert my eyes, just following the direction of their footsteps, but the commander in charge of my unit saw my pain and said I needed to steel myself, that this is war and I needed to get used to it. He put a sword in my hand and ordered me to kill one of the children that was trapped in the rubble."

"…and did you?" the Thoron asked, holding his breath, almost afraid to hear the answer.

"No," he replied, "I refused. I told him I was just a healer and fighting wasn't my job, but he said that every soldier should have blood on their hands and shoved the sword back at me. He dragged me to the child and threw me down in front of him. 'Do it!' he yelled, 'Kill him, or you'll die beside him.' Looking into his eyes was like looking into the eyes of evil itself. There was this sinister look of joy in them like he was enjoying the thought of forcing me to taint my hands with blood. It sent a chill down my spine and in that moment, I knew it wasn't an empty threat. He would kill me, and he would enjoy every second of it. I didn't know what to do, I was trembling so much I could barely hold the sword. I stood in front of the child, contemplating if this was the moment I would die. I tried to lift the sword, but I couldn't bring myself to do it. Looking into that boy's eyes, I couldn't harm him, regardless of the cost. My people were born with the ability to heal the injured, not cause them harm. I dropped the sword and as I did, a loud crash thundered above us. A large piece of a building came tumbling down between me and the rest of my unit. When the dust cleared, I realized the boy had also been crushed by the falling debris. I tried to move some rubble out of the way to find him but when I got a glimpse of his face, I knew he was already lost. With the path to my unit cut off, I realized it was now or never. Become a murderer, a martyr, or a fugitive. I chose the latter. I ran to the southern end of town as fast as I could, trying to avoid falling debris and the like. I ran through what felt like an ocean of corpses and it tore my heart in two, knowing there was nothing I could do for them. I occasionally stopped when I thought one might still be breathing, but to no avail. Along the way south I did, however, find a boy holding his bleeding mother. I couldn't bring myself to run past, I had to stop. She had clearly been pierced by arrows during one of the volleys sent over the wall. He begged me to help her and I assured him I'd do everything I could. I slowly removed the arrows one by one, using my powers to close each wound as I pulled the arrows free. She passed out from the pain before I could finish. When the last of them was removed I closed the final wound and watched as a wave of relief washed over her face. I tried to wake her but she was exhausted from the trauma. I pulled her into a nearby home that was open and told the boy to watch over her."

"Did you ask their names?" Chronol asked.

"I didn't," he replied. "Truth be told, I had no belief that they would survive the night. The Kohtans were very clear on the rules of engagement for this battle. For the first time they would take no prisoners or conscripts from the attack. They believed the Thorons too dangerous to be left alive and if taken into the military or taken as slaves, they would one day rise up and fight back from inside the empire. They wanted to squash any possibility of a rebellion and so they intended on killing all of them, but even knowing this, I couldn't let that boy watch his mother slowly bleed out in his arms. I did what I could and ran, continuing south until I found the exit. There were a few Kohtan soldiers posted at that end but I was able to convince them that my unit had been killed and I was trying to escape back to the main encampment so I could recover and be assigned to a new unit. If not for this brand on my neck they probably would've killed me on sight. Funny how the mark that saved me is now the mark that forever condemns me as a deserter. Regardless, once I made it out of the city, I ran for my life and eventually ended up here. I've been hiding out here ever since. I found a kind farmer on the west side of town who understood my plight and took me in. I'm staying with him until I can figure out a more permanent solution. I might try my luck at heading east and seeing if I can make my way into the Kingdom of Caldor. I understand they maintain a peaceful domain and are willing to take in refugees like myself who are trying to escape from the empire. Only time will tell if that's true or not."

"I see," Chronol nodded, scratching his chin. He finally released the pressure from Vaelin's foot, allowing it free.

"Oh thank you," he sighed, "I'd lost feeling in it some time ago but I dared not ask to be released."

"I'm sorry," Chronol apologized, "I thought you a fiend and couldn't risk you revealing my identity. After hearing your story, I realize you are in many ways just as much a victim here as myself. It would seem I was wrong to some degree about the Kohtan army. Not everyone who dawns the uniform is necessarily the villain I imagined. Is there any way to tell them apart? Conscripts from volunteers..."

"Yes, actually," he replied, "there is one obvious difference. Those who volunteer aren't branded, they are instead given a medallion with the military emblem on it. Those of us taken by force are branded. This is the easiest way to tell apart the different soldiers in the army."

"I see," Chronol acknowledged. "This is very useful information, thank you."

"Do not be fooled," Vaelin warned. "Yes, there are many conscripts who are of the same mind as myself and want nothing to do with the military, but many are corrupted by the ones who bind us. I've watched good people turn into the very monsters that enslaved us. Not all who carry the brand are innocents, do not let your guard down. Ever..."

"Thank you, again," Chronol nodded, shaking his hand. "I appreciate everything you shared with me. You've given me a lot to think about. What about that boy and his mother? Any idea where they might have escaped off to?"

"The afterlife I would assume," he replied solemnly. "I can't imagine they made it out of that city. He was far too small to carry her and she was in no condition to run. They wouldn't have stood a chance once they were found and it was only a matter of time until the soldiers would sweep that area for survivors. I can only hope that they were able to enjoy what few moments they had left with each other in peace and that those monsters ended their lives swiftly. I wouldn't hold out any hope of finding any survivors if I were you. They may be savages but they're quite thorough." Chronol looked down, seemingly disheartened by the response. "I'm sorry, sir. I don't mean to be negative, just being realistic. I don't want you to get your hopes up on finding survivors and potentially put yourself in further danger, just to find someone who's not out there. Look at how you put yourself in harm's way coming into the town thinking you had found a single survivor. You could be found out by any of the patrolling guards and possibly be captured and killed over someone who wasn't even one of your kin. I just want you to move forward with the knowledge that you are likely the last of your kind and you should be careful wherever you go. They will send soldiers after you if they find out a Thoron survived the battle. Your best bet at safety is to keep your identity to yourself and stay as far away from the military as possible. Maybe you should make for Caldor as well. You have no brand, nothing to mark you as Kohtan, they'd likely let you into their borders."

"Perhaps," Chronol replied, Vaelin's words still echoing in his ears. "Perhaps..."

"Are you alright?" Vaelin asked. His eyes seemed to flicker with magic for a moment as he looked Chronol over.

"I'm fine..." he responded. "Thank you for the information. I should be going. I'm sorry for detaining you, please be careful out there." He bowed his head slightly and left the table, immediately heading out the door and out of the city to the woods north of town. "You are likely the last of your kind..." Those words continued to echo in his mind as he walked through the forest.

When night fell, he climbed into a tree and laid with his wolfhound, holding him against his chest. He silently stared into the darkness for hours, listening to the leaves rustle in the gentle breeze. His mind felt numb as he absorbed everything the Weaver had shared with him and trying to process it all meant sleep would most likely elude him that evening. The only sound to escape his lips all night was one sentence.

"Am I really all that's left?"

6

The Homeless

Dawn crept through the leaves around Chronol, shining light on his already open eyes, wrapping around his face and caressing his now bearded chin. He looked down at Maksis who still slept peacefully on his chest. Petting his fur softly, Chronol gently woke up the small wolfhound. His brown and silver eyes slowly opened; his eyelids heavy as he tried to wake. The pup stretched out his little body and let out a big yawn. Rolling over onto his paws, he stood up and shook off the remaining sleepiness, immediately climbing up his master and licking his face. Chronol pet him gently, scratching behind his ears and nodding quietly. He scooped up the little wolfhound and tucked him away in his pouch before climbing down from his tree. Safely back on the ground, he let the pup run and hop around a bit while scoping out the area around him. Making their way quietly, Chronol's eyes stayed intently focused on the area around him, looking for the smallest indication of movement. After some searching, he noticed a small bit of rustling in the nearby brush and threw his dagger at the source, instantly pinning down and killing the little animal. Retrieving the kill, he quickly skinned it and fed it to Maksis, then caught another for himself. When they were both fed he took Maks out a ways and let him run around in a small clearing, tossing a twig for the wolfhound to chase and play with. When the pup was finished exercising, they made their way back to the same tree and climbed back up, laying in the same place as the night before. There he'd lay, waiting for the following morning. It had been several weeks since his encounter with the Kohtan deserter, but he hadn't moved beyond the same tree he hid in that night. Day after day the same routine; never changing, never moving forward, never speaking. Chronol's face looked emotionless, empty, like a puppet being manipulated from one chore to the next. No life or motivation to anything he did. Weeks turned into months and Chronol remained in the same area, seeming to move through his days like a man with no soul. Night after night, he looked back at the day that brought him to this point. The day that changed his world forever. Wondering what he could've done differently, what he could've done to save his city, or even just a handful of people. Why did he have to be alone? Why was he the only survivor? Asking those questions yet again, he drifted off to sleep, his mind replaying the events of the day of the battle.

It was a morning like any other. The sun warmed the city as Chronol awoke from his slumber. After bathing and getting dressed in his usual training outfit, he sat down and had a hearty breakfast, leaving a small plate of food on the floor which was gobbled up by a tiny little hound under his chair. When they finished eating, he grabbed his sword and headed out, leaving the pup in charge of guarding the house. He walked across town, greeting the familiar faces on the street as he passed by. The pretty blonde from the flower shop tossed him a rose, waving and giving him a playful wink when he looked her way. He smiled bashfully, nodding and thanking her for the flower, then continued on his way until there was a tug on his belt. Looking down he found Milus, one of the children of the town, holding a little baby dragon.

"Hello, Milus," he grinned. "What's that you have there?"

"Zalluun had a baby," the boy smiled, holding up the little dragon. "Look how cute she is!"

"My word, that's quite a beautiful dragon," he nodded, inspecting it. Her wings looked strong for a newborn and her scales were a bright, vibrant red. "She looks like she'll be quite the flyer one day."

"You think so?" the boy asked, looking over the baby, trying to see what Chronol saw.

"I'm sure we'll find out in time," he smiled, rustling the boy's hair. "I've got an appointment with Toronil, so I need to be heading out. I'll check in on you two later. Don't keep that baby away from her mother for too long."

"Alright," the boy agreed. "I'll take her back to Zalluun now. I'll see you later!" he waved and then headed off toward the hatchery to return the baby to its mother. Chronol continued towards the barracks and headed to the training area in the back. There were a few other soldiers working with practice dummies, while others sparred with each other. Entering the practice arena, he heard a voice from behind him shout "On guard!" Chronol drew his blade, quickly turning around and clashed his sword with that of a young man smiling as he pulled away, his light brown hair drifting into his face for a moment during the retreat.

"Quick reflexes as always, I see," the young man grinned, his blue eyes peeking playfully through the hair covering them. "I thought I finally had the jump on you."

"Did you plan on cleaving me in half with that surprise attack?" Chronol laughed, attacking the man. Their swords clashed, strike after strike, as Chronol backed his attacker towards the fence. He stopped his assault just before the man ran out of room to back away. "You'll get better with time, Toronil, of that I am certain. But never sacrifice your honor in a duel. When a man is willing to lay down his advantages in battle and face you one on one, you owe them the courtesy of an honorable duel."

"I know, sir," nodded Toronil. "I'm sorry for the surprise attack. If I thought I had even a remote chance of actually getting the drop on you, I never would have done it."

"It's alright," Chronol smiled. "You're still new to the military, I know you'll learn everything you need to know in time." He brought his sword up to the ready, beckoning Toronil to attack. "Now then, shall we continue your instruction?"

"Yes, sir," the young soldier smiled, preparing his blade and coming in for another attack. The two sparred for some time, going back and forth from defense to offense while Chronol instructed him on different methods of attack and defense, taking advantage of their abilities as Thorons while remaining mindful of the potential side effects of those techniques. When they finished, Chronol bid his student farewell and headed out through the city gates. He searched around the fields south of town for a bit before finding what he was looking for: a little, purple flower so small and delicate it can only survive off in the woods where it can't be harmed by passersby. They bloom so rarely that most people don't know they exist, but he discovered them on his last patrol around the city. He carefully picked one, wrapping it gently in a cloth from his pouch. With flower in hand, he headed back to town. On the walk there, he passed by the flower stall and placed the cloth on the counter.

"Good afternoon, Saelina," he smiled. "I found this recently and thought you'd like it."

"Did you now?" she grinned, a look of curiosity in her eyes as she unwrapped the flower. Her eyes lit up and a big smile crept across her face. "This is beautiful," she said, looking up at him. "Wherever did you find it?"

"There's a small clearing in the woods south of here," he explained. "I came across it during one of my patrols and thought I'd get one for you the next time you were working." She brought it to her nose and smelled it softly. The aroma was sweet and pleasant, not too overwhelming or potent and seemed to fill her with a sense of relaxation.

"It's lovely, thank you so much," she said softly. "I hope it wasn't too much trouble to retrieve."

"Not at all," he assured her. "I was happy to bring such a delicate thing to someone who I knew would truly appreciate it." She smiled as they shared a moment of silence, just looking at each other. "Well, then," Chronol spoke up, "I should be on my way. I need to get cleaned up before my patrol." He bowed his head slightly towards the young woman and stepped back. "Enjoy the flower and have a wonderful day." With that, he turned and started to walk away.

"Be safe out there," she called out to him, holding the flower close, "and thank you again." She watched him wave over his shoulder, then closed her eyes and breathed in the aroma once more. When he arrived home and opened the door, a little ball of fur quickly scampered past him and went straight into the nearby grass.

"I'm sorry, little one," he apologized. The little pup found a place nearby and relieved himself. "My errands took a little longer than expected. I didn't mean to leave you for so long." When the hound had finished, he ran back inside and waited for his master. "You must be hungry, let me get you something to eat." He placed some food on Maks's plate and left the little wolfhound to enjoy his meal, then went to go get himself cleaned up. While drying himself off, a sound that he had not heard in a very long time brought his quiet evening to an abrupt end.

Diiinnnggg…..Diiinnnggg…..Diiinnnggg…..Diiinnnggg…..

"Is that the warning bell…?" Chronol thought for a moment, almost convinced it couldn't possibly be. The bell had not been rung in years as no one has dared to attack the city. But as he listened, the warning bell continued to ring throughout the city. "Something must be seriously wrong for them to ring that bell… I'd better hurry." He quickly finished dressing, putting on his uniform and armor and grabbing his sword and shield. With unnatural speed he raced through the town, rushing towards the guard post where the warning bell was being rung. Upon his arrival he dashed up the tower to where the soldier was ringing the bell. "Norinth, what's the meaning of this? What's going o…" Before he could finish his question, movement in the fields east of the city drew his attention. What was once a verdant ocean of green was now being consumed by a wave of black pouring in from over the hill. The faint sound of marching could be heard as more and more soldiers poured in over the horizon. "What is the meaning of this…? Are we under attack?" Chronol thought for a moment and then snapped back to his senses, remembering his training for such a situation. "Norinth, enough with that bell! Get this gate closed immediately!" He looked over to a young dragon that sat on a perch just outside the guard tower. "Uurith," he called out. His voice seemed to echo and reverberate. "Launch the signal flame for the others to close their gates." The dragon nodded its head then faced upward, opening its mouth and shooting a flame up into the air. A minute later, other flames around the city shot up in response, as the various city gates began to close. After seeing this, he quickly climbed back down and headed for the barracks. He found a mass of soldiers preparing themselves for combat, grabbing supplies and falling in with their respective units. Chronol was immediately approached by another soldier with a similar uniform to his own.

"I'm glad you're here," he greeted, grabbing Chronol by the shoulder. "I needed to convey Zerahl's orders before heading out with my men."

"Of course, Rayz," Chronol nodded, "Just tell me where you want my men dispatched. Where's the commander headed?"

"Zerahl's taking his men to run through the inner perimeter of the city to make sure all guards know their orders and most civilians are out of harm's way before they man the eastern gate. I'm taking my regiment to the north gate and you and your men are in charge of the south gate."

"It shall be done, my friend," Chronol agreed, grabbing Rayz' shoulder and nodding. "Our men will stand strong no matter what the enemy throws our way, isn't that right men?" he called out to his troops. They all shouted and cheered in agreement, rapidly banging swords to shields. This display enlivened the rest of the soldiers, causing them to break out into battle cries as well. Rayz smiled and let out a small sigh of relief, seeing his men ready for combat.

"Very well, let us be off then," said Rayz. "Kaaldoth's strength be with you and your men."

"To you and yours as well," Chronol replied. "We'll see you after the battle."

The two groups went their separate ways. Chronol led his men to their position near the south gate, taking the time before the attack to go through his regiment one by one, making sure each man was focused and ready to fight. At sunset, the sound of thunderous footsteps could be heard outside the city. The invading army approached, getting louder and louder the closer they marched. Before long they were upon the city, banging at the gates. A group of Thorons up on the wall began firing arrows down into the sea of attacking soldiers. The army retaliated, firing a storm of arrows in return. One by one the archers on the wall fell as wave after wave of arrows rained upon them. The enemy arrows covered so much of the area that Chronol's regiment had to back away from the gate, unable to stand adjacent to it without being swarmed by arrows. Awaiting their enemy's entry, they heard the distant crank of wood and metal. Ballista bolts and giant stones began to fly over the wall, piercing soldiers and destroying buildings.

"Hold your ground, men!" Chronol shouted. "This side of the city doesn't fall unless we do! Our lives in the service of Thoros! Fight to protect those that you love! Fight to protect your honor! Fight to protect your homes! Fight to protect our freedom! FIGHT! FIGHT! FIGHT!" As he shouted, his soldiers began to chant alongside him, preparing for the onrush of soldiers to pour through the gate. While they chanted, a wave of dragons took to the skies, leaving the city. Bursts of light could be seen over the wall as roars of flames burned the attackers. Suddenly, the gate began to crack and snap, until it finally burst open. A swarm of invaders poured through the gates, rushing towards the soldiers. Wave after wave of men came crashing against Thoron shields, each one being dispatched with minimal Thoron casualties. For every hundred that came through, another two or three Thorons would fall. Feeling the momentum of the battle was on their side, the defenders continued to stand their ground, confident their superior battle skills and physical ability would see them through to victory.

But the waves of enemies continued with no end in sight, and when they wouldn't fall fast enough, the enemy began firing volleys of arrows into the fray, hitting both Thoron and ally alike. The Thorons began to take losses more quickly and needed to fall back to get distance between themselves and the archers. The battle became more chaotic when the invaders began throwing torches into the nearby homes, setting the city ablaze. The very sky itself seemed to crackle with lightning, and fire rained down casting streaks of light across Chronol's armor. Battle cries were heard over the sounds of swords and shields clashing. The thunderous crash of falling stone, as walls collapsed and buildings crumbled, was deafening. Piercing through the chaos was the sound of a child crying. "What're you doing out here? You need to get inside NOW!" Chronol cried out. The child looked at him, tears streaming from his eyes; a small, wooden toy horse clutched in his hand. The boy screamed. Chronol's eyes grew wide; he reached out, time seeming to slow down. The cold, iron ballista bolt crept through the air, growing closer to the boy. With a flash of blinding speed, Chronol dashed forward, putting himself in front of the boy. A splash of red sprayed forth before his eyes. He looked down, seeing the tip of the blood-soaked bolt coming out of his chest. "Daran... run..." he coughed, blood pouring from his mouth. The boy turned and ran down an alley as Chronol collapsed to the floor, a pool of his own blood forming around him. Through blurred vision, he watched his soldiers fall one by one.

Chronol woke up gasping for air. Wrapped by the branches that he'd been hiding in for the past few months, he looked around and realized his surroundings. This dream was more vivid and detailed than any other he'd had since the battle. His hand felt his chest and for the first time in months, Chronol spoke out loud. "I... died?" The scene from his dream replayed in his head again and again and each time he became more and more convinced that the bolt had pierced him through the chest. "It can't be... it must be just something I dreamed. I'm here, I couldn't have died..." He tried to get it out of his head but it was all he thought about all day long. By nightfall his mind was splitting in two trying to figure out if what he saw was real or not. He remembered there being a gash in the front of his armor but he never had any reason to check the back. For all he knew it could've just been a slash from a sword or something of the like. "I can't deal with this... I need to know. Tomorrow, we'll start heading back to where I buried my armor. The truth will be there," he explained to Maksis. The wolfhound tilted his head to the side, then curled up in a ball and went to sleep. "I'm glad you're as perplexed by this as I am," Chronol sighed. "But you're right, if we're traveling tomorrow we best get some sleep. Goodnight, pup."

As decided, when morning came Chronol left his tree and began the journey back towards Thoros, hoping to find the spot in the woods where he buried his armor. His ability to keep watch of his surroundings seemed impared as his mind raced with flashes of his dream from the night before. It was the first time he'd remembered so much detail of that night. "But was it a dream or a memory?" Chronol thought to himself. "How could it be real? It's not possible." These thoughts plagued his mind day after day as he tried to carefully backtrack through the woods that would bring him home to Thoros. With each day he got closer to his destination, and each day his stomach seemed to turn a little more. It was unclear if his discomfort came from heading back towards the ones that destroyed his home, or confronting the proof of whether what he dreamt was real or not.

Finally, after some traveling and searching, Chronol found a little shift in the brush that he recognized to be the camouflage left to hide where the armor was buried. Quickly beginning to dig, his little companion following suit beside him. Shoveling the dirt away with his hands, Chronol started feeling like he'd been digging for hours. "Was this the right place? Did someone find it? Am I just slowly losing my mind?" These thoughts began floating through his mind as Chronol grew more and more worried until his fingers finally hit something hard, causing him to freeze for a moment. What was once fast, almost manic digging, became a slow, cautious excavation, as if Chronol was afraid to find the answer he'd so desperately been searching for just moments ago. Lifting it from the earth, dirt fell away and revealed the hidden armor. The chest had a large cut through it just like he remembered, and when he slowly turned it around, his eyes saw the truth of that night. An equally large gash in the back; clearly made from something piercing through the front and back of the armor. There was no more denying it.

"No... it can't be true..." Chronol whispered. "No... I died... I died? I can't have died... I'm here. I'm alive... and alone..." Tears began to stream from his eyes. "It can't be true... it's not fair. How did I come back? Was it that weaver? Did he heal me? No, if that was the case he would have recognized me. How then? How did I survive? Was it one of the other conscripts? I don't understand... Why am I alive?? IT ISN'T FAIR! I SHOULD BE DEAD LIKE EVERYONE ELSE!" he cried, throwing the armor against a nearby tree. "I don't want to be alive! This isn't fair! Why must I bear this curse! What happened to me?" Looking at the armor slumped against the tree, a small plate of metal reflected the green glow in his eyes. "Is that why my eyes are like this?? I didn't ask for this! I just want it to be over! Please... I don't want this life..." He fell face down onto the ground, crying into the dirt. "I don't want to be alone... I don't want to keep going... please let me die..." Chronol laid there till the crying subsided. His eyes were dull and lifeless as they stared off to the side. A soft whimpering next to him disturbed his silence. Maksis crawled over to his face, licking his nose. "No..." he replied quietly. "Just go... you can take care of yourself, you don't need me. Please, just go. I just want to lay here till I die..." The pup continued whining, biting and tugging at his master's shirt, trying to pull him. "No, I said," he sighed. "Go away, leave me alone. You'll be fine on your own, leave me." He gently reached up and pushed Maksis away. The hound looked at his master, still whining. Chronol closed his eyes, not wanting to see the pup's face. Some time passed before tiny paws could be heard wandering off a little ways. "Good… you'll be better off without me…" he thought to himself.

Hours passed in silence while Chronol lay there speechless, motionless, thoughtless, and alone. His mind was an empty void, embracing the silence, waiting for everything to finally be over. Late that night the quiet was disturbed by a familiar yelp in the distance. Chronol's eyes shot open and looked in the direction of the sound. Maksis could be heard crying in the nearby trees. "No, Maks!" He quickly got up and ran towards the sound. Maksis was leaned on one side, biting at his own paw. "What happened? Let me see," he said, trying to calm the hound. Looking the paw over he realized Maksis had stepped on a long thorn that pierced his paw. "That has to hurt," he said, trying to gently pull it out. Maksis cried out, gently biting at his master's hand. "Easy, boy," he reassured. "I know it hurts, I have to get this out. Just try to relax, I'll make it quick." He took a moment to let the wolfhound calm down before continuing. In one quick motion, he pulled the thorn from the paw. Maksis let out a loud yelp and Chronol quickly let the hound free. Maks licked his paw, whimpering from the pain. "I'm sorry, boy…" he apologized. "This is my fault… I shouldn't have left you to wander on your own like that." The pup limped over to his master, crawling up on his lap and laying on his back like a baby. Chronol picked him up and cradled him, sitting back against a tree, staring at the little life in his arms. "Maybe you need me after all…" he thought to himself. Sitting there holding his little wolfhound, he realized he still had a purpose to fulfill. There was still one life for him to protect and care for. With that in mind, it was time for him to decide where they would go from here.

7

The Traveler

Morning came to find Chronol and his wolfhound still huddled together against the same tree from the previous night. The green glow of the Thoron's eyes shone through the shadow of the tree as he sat there, having found no sleep. His night spent in thought, trying to figure out what to do from this point. Until now, the idea of finding other survivors was all that drove him, all that guided his actions. With that dream now faded away, he needed to find a new path to follow. He thought back to the conversation he overheard in Eppildor. The talk of a peaceful kingdom beyond the borders of The Kohtan Empire sounded almost like a fairytale. But the more he weighed his options, the more it seemed like his best choice was to head east in search of this kingdom. Staying anywhere within the borders of the empire would prove most dangerous, keeping him forever on the run as a fugitive, endangering those around him. If this kingdom really is all they say it is, it would be the closest civilization to that of Thoros that he'd be able to find.

"I've come so far west again, the trek east will take some time and I'm bound to run into some patrols along the way," he thought to himself. "But if that's what it takes to keep you safe, little one, then that's what we'll do. We'll make our way to the outskirts of the empire's control and see if such a land truly exists. Worst that could happen, no one controls it and it's just wildlands. Even then, we'd at least be out of their reach and could make some semblance of a life in the wilderness," he pondered, smiling at the little ball of fur starting to stir and wake up in his arms. "We'll be alright, you'll see. I'll keep you safe." Chronol looked towards the north, knowing the city that was once his home was just beyond the forest. "Shall we look upon it once more before we leave? I don't expect we'll ever see it again…" The pup woke and stretched, shaking off the sleepiness and pawing at its master's chest. "Alright little one, up we go." He tucked the pup back into the pouch, the once loose fit now becoming a bit tight, leaving Maksis' head sticking out of the top. "You're getting too big for this," he smiled, "We're going to have to teach you how to climb soon." The hound barked softly, seeming to respond to his master's comment. Chronol made his way up the tree, climbing until he could see over the canopy of the forest. Looking north, he saw the place he had called home for so many years. The Kohtan banners waved proudly between the now decomposing bodies of his fallen allies. He averted his gaze, somewhat regretting his decision to see this sight once more. Steeling himself to look again, he stared on, reminding himself of the horror that awaited him if he was found and using that to strengthen his motivation to flee. "Say goodbye, little one." After a final look he turned away, climbing down to the ground and heading east. He let Maksis loose to walk alongside him, keeping a constant eye out for any patrols that might be in the area.

Days passed in this manner as they journeyed farther and farther from Thoros. However, just when he thought they were far enough to let his guard down a little, he spotted what appeared to be a patrol coming his way. They were too close for him to make it up a tree without being seen, so he ducked into some nearby bushes, doing his best not to disturb his surroundings. He quickly whispered to the pup, instructing him to sit and stay in the brush beside his master and watched for their approach. A few moments later he could hear them getting closer. He listened to them speak of different advantages they had as Kohtan military. Inspecting the soldiers one by one, he noticed a medallion hung around the necks of all but one of them. One younger man in the group had a brand on his neck. "A conscript…" he thought to himself, remembering his conversation with Vaelin. They continued walking, one of the soldiers bragging about a woman he took advantage of in town. "She clearly wanted it," he laughed. Chronol's eyes flared so brightly he felt compelled to close them, fearing they'd be seen. He gritted his teeth, trying to refrain from engaging the group. Regaining his composure, he opened his eyes to see the young man with the brand laughing along with the rest of the soldiers. "Do not be fooled… many are corrupted by the ones who bind us. I've watched good people turn into the very monsters that enslaved us. Not all who carry the brand are innocents…" Vaelin's words echoed in his mind. Chronol shook his head and remained silent, waiting for the patrol to pass. When it was safe to move, he left his place of hiding, calling for Maksis and continuing his journey east.

His mind was filled with thoughts of the soldiers that had passed by. "Why do they all seem so corrupt? So evil… What do the Kohtans do to their children to raise them into such cruel, immoral beings? Whatever it is, it seems to spread and infect those they enslave. I feel for that young man. Something tells me he wasn't always like that. Nevertheless, it seems he's fallen victim to their plague. We truly need to get as far away from this place as possible." Day after day, Chronol continued his trek eastward, avoiding the occasional military patrol, doing his best not to engage them.

His journey continued this way until the day he encountered a group he couldn't bring himself to avoid. It started with the sound of laughter. Chronol could hear there was a group of people up ahead, too loud and rowdy to be a Kohtan patrol. Carefully, he approached the noise and saw what looked like a group of bandits clad in black and silver. They were advancing toward a woman who was on her knees by a campfire, shaking an unconscious man, his black hair slick with blood. Her hazel eyes could be seen peering through her light brown hair, tears streaming from them as she tried to wake the man up. Everything seemed to slow down for a moment. Chronol's glowing eyes flared at the sight. He immediately wanted to intervene and save the couple, but the memory of his last fight flashed through his mind. The look on the faces of those he'd saved, the absolute horror at his display of savagery, seemed to paralyze him for a moment. Knowing he never wanted to fall into that level of rage again, he closed his eyes for a brief moment and did his best to control his emotional state. With a deep breath he opened his eyes, the glow in them now more stable than before, and drew his sword. "I am not a monster…" he whispered to himself, sprinting into the clearing. He shouted as he closed in, trying to draw their attention away from the woman. The bandits suddenly turned to see an unknown swordsman charging them from the treeline. Those who were unarmed quickly drew their weapons. He dashed through the middle of them, deflecting two of their attacks and positioning himself between the couple and the thieves. "STOP!" he commanded, standing before them, his sword glittering in the sunlight. "Leave these people at once. Sheath your weapons and you may leave peacefully." The thieves looked puzzled, seeing this stranger who was clearly outnumbered six to one making demands like he actually held the advantage. They began to laugh once more, slowly stalking towards him. "HALT!" he shouted. "This is your final warning! I don't want to hurt you!"

His plea fell on deaf ears as they continued to find humor in his ultimatum. The one closest to him lunged in for an attack. He parried the strike, knocking his attacker's sword to the side then knocking it from his hand. Chronol suddenly dashed forward, slamming his knee into the bandit's stomach, sending him reeling to the floor, unable to breath. The others, seeing this display, were immediately sent into a rage of vengeance. They charged the mysterious swordsman, yelling and shouting. Chronol blocked and parried each attack, attempting to restrain himself and avoid any lethal hits. It was like a bird trying not to fly, his training and instincts telling him where to strike and counter to quickly end the threat, but his mind doing everything to override his reflexes and keep his attackers alive. One by one he began disabling them, cracking one of them across the jaw with the hilt of his sword, knocking him unconscious. Another attacked and he dodged to the side, kicking this one in the back and sending him slamming into a tree. The remaining three seemed better coordinated in their attacks, keeping him on the defensive. Eventually, one of them made a mistake and left himself open to a counterattack. Every muscle in Chronol's body wanted to immediately go for a finishing blow, but he held back, attempting to kick the man in the head. The thief ducked below the attack, countering with a blade across his attacker's back. Chronol's eyes flashed a brilliant green and he turned towards the one that cut him. The thieves were visibly startled by the sight, their attacks becoming uncoordinated as they tried to make sense of what they were seeing. Chronol fought against his instincts, but still countered with a savage strike on one of the thieves, severing off his hand. The man screamed in pain, holding his bleeding wrist. The other two were distracted by the terrible sight, leaving them open to Chronol's attacks, so he immediately went on the offensive with a barrage of sword strikes. They were pushed back until he was able to disarm one, knocking the bandit's sword upward and lodging it into a tree branch overhead. He followed up by grabbing the disarmed man by the face and slamming his head into that of his ally. With a loud crack of bone impacting bone, the two of them slumped to the floor, knocked out on top of each other. He approached the thief whose hand he had severed. The bandit sat there on the ground, holding his wrist, shouting as he stared at the void where his hand used to be. Chronol walked up and punched the man in the face, knocking him unconscious.

With the fight finally over, the woman who had been holding the unconscious man all this time, called out to Chronol. "Sir? I'm not sure where you came from but thank you." She watched the swordsman, who seemed unphased by her statement, grab the shirt of one of the bandits and tear it. Going to the injured man, he wrapped the end of the arm where he had cut off his hand. "What're you doing?" she asked.

Chronol pulled the thief's belt from his waist, beginning to wrap it tightly around the wounded wrist. "Trying to save him from bleeding out," he finally responded.

"But... why?" she asked. "These monsters attacked my husband for attempting to defend my honor. Why bother saving them?"

"Because..." he explained, "everyone deserves a chance at redemption." He finished dressing the wound and tore fabric from another bandit's shirt, walking towards the couple. "Please," he asked, "allow me to tend to his wounds." She nodded and Chronol took a look at her husband. "He should be alright," he assured her, "let's get him patched up to be sure. So, what exactly happened here?" he asked, while tending to her husband. Maksis scurried over and sat beside his master, watching him mend the man's wound.

"A wolfhound?" she said curiously. "Hello there, little pup. He must be yours?" Chronol nodded, continuing with his task. "I see. Well," she continued, "my husband and I are traveling bards. We go from town to town sharing tales and singing songs for gold. We were making our way towards Biridon when we were stopped by these bandits. They insisted we needed to pay a toll to travel this road. When we refused, they suggested taking me for the evening as payment. My husband stood his ground, demanding an apology for insulting my honor. They responded by striking him over the head. It seemed they were about to get what they wanted when you arrived. Truly, I can only imagine what they would have done to us had you not saved us when you did. You are truly a skilled swordsman."

"I'll have to practice this new fighting style if I want to survive an encounter like this again," he replied, shifting his shoulder, feeling the cut sting across his back. "I'm just glad the two of you are alright," he smiled and finished bandaging the man's head. "It may take him a little while to come to, and I can't very well leave you with these fiends here just waiting to wake up…." He looked over to the bodies of the unconscious bandits, trying to think of a solution to his dilemma. "This is certainly easier when they're all dead…" he whispered to himself.

"What was that?" she asked.

"Nothing," he replied, "just thinking out loud." He began collecting the bodies and sitting them in a circle around a tree. He searched the area and found a group of horses that clearly belonged to the thieves. Upon further investigation he found a coil of rope on the side of one of the horses and used it to bind the bandits to the tree. "This should keep them in place for a while." He searched them, looking through their belongings, and noticed each of them had a silver medallion of what looked like a crescent moon. Unfamiliar with the symbol, he continued to search them, eventually finding their coin pouches. He took some money from each bag and placed it into one pouch. Returning to the horses, he unleashed one from the tree it was tied to and brought it to the couple, tying the bag of gold to the side of the horse. The woman's husband slowly began opening his eyes just as Chronol approached. "Here, this should help compensate you for your trouble," he said, offering her the reins. "Take the horse and continue your journey. This lot shouldn't be able to get out of those ropes for quite a while, buying you more than enough time to get away from here." Her husband was slowly shaking his head, trying to clear his vision and get a grasp of his surroundings.

"What happened?" he asked, looking up to his wife.

"We were rescued," she explained. "You're alright, that's all that matters. And we have this kind stranger to thank for it," she said, looking up, expecting to see Chronol. To her surprise, he was already walking away towards the woods to the east. "Wait! Sir! Please, tell us your name, that we might sing the ballad of the brave warrior who saved our lives!" Chronol shook his head, waving to them without stopping.

"I'm no one of importance. Take care of each other and have a safe journey," he said, heading back into the trees with Maksis scampering along behind him.

"But..." she sighed. "Saving us and not wanting any credit for it. He truly does deserve to be immortalized in song. But without a name... Well, glowing green eyes and a wolfhound, that's still quite the unique description. I suppose that'll have to do."

Chronol continued his journey, thinking of the look on the woman's face. No fear, no terror, just gratitude. It filled him with a sense of peace and fulfillment, knowing he had saved them without losing himself in a state of rage. He would hold onto that feeling while he traveled, journeying further from home than he had ever been before. He passed through unfamiliar lands until he eventually found himself confronted with what looked like a stone pillar just beyond the end of the forest. He kept to the shadows of the woods, inspecting the pillar from a distance. There were a few horses tied off at the base of the structure and some guards at the top, watching the surrounding area. It was then that Chronol realized this was a guard tower. In that instant, fear gripped him thinking he had found some far off Kohtan guard post, but the color scheme and emblems on the horses were not that of the Kohtan empire. "These must be soldiers from the Kingdom of Caldor" he thought to himself. "But if they see me, they'll likely think I'm a Kohtan spy or something of the sort. I need to find a spot where I can get through undetected." He made his way south until he eventually found another Caldorian guard tower. "With a spyglass, one could see about halfway from one tower to the other, indicating these towers are spaced the maximum distance apart to limit overlap. It'd be a bit too dangerous to pass during the daylight. I could make it through under cover of darkness if I wait till tonight. I should keep an eye on these soldiers. If they're good enough to keep the Kohtans at bay, I'm sure they're smart enough to send out night patrols to compensate for the distance and darkness between their towers. I'll wait and look for an opening to pass through."

He waited in the trees near the center of the two towers until nightfall. His prediction was confirmed when a couple soldiers came out of each tower and began patrolling between the structures, carrying torches to illuminate the darkness. To their credit, the pattern they patrolled in made it very difficult to find any hole in their observation. After about an hour, Chronol found there was a brief moment where he could pass between two of the guards unnoticed, but the window of opportunity was so small that he'd need to be as close as possible before making his move. Scooping up Maksis, he crept quietly through the darkness, moving closer to the patrolled area and stopped at his intended hiding spot. Kneeling in the shadow of a small boulder just on the edge of where the soldier's light could reach, Chronol watched and waited, biding his time for the proper moment. After another round of patrols, he prepared himself to move and then dashed towards the gap in their defenses when his window of opportunity opened. With blinding speed he slipped through the patrol line, dropping to the ground and laying flat on the other side of the border. The patrol continued their route, seemingly unaware of his presence. He waited for the next short gap to be able to get up and hurry deeper into Caldorian territory.

Finally, he was outside the influence of the Empire. He knelt in the nearby trees, putting Maksis down so the hound could move freely. He scratched the little pup's ears, his eyes feeling unusually heavy. "We made it, little one. We're free…" With the last of his strength, Chronol trekked a bit further into the woods, then climbed a tree and closed his eyes. Tomorrow the sunrise of a new land would wake him. With that thought in mind, he fell into a deep sleep, finally looking forward to a new day.

8

The Foreigner

The morning sun crept over the horizon while the shade of tree branches cradled the sleeping Thoron and wolfhound. For the first time in the months since his home was destroyed, neither Chronol nor his companion stirred at dawn. Both of them remained still; calm and peaceful as if a weight had been lifted from their shoulders. Hours passed before the swordsman slowly opened his eyes; they were still heavy, unaccustomed to this much sleep. His body felt like stone, not wanting to move. He shook his head, trying to break free from the sleepiness weighing him down. Opening his eyes wider and running his fingers through his hair, he finally started to feel a little more coherent. He poured a few drops of water from his waterskin into his hands and rubbed his face, the cool liquid washing away the last of his sleepiness. "Well then," he thought to himself. "It would seem we've made it into this country's territory, now what?" He gently woke the wolfhound on his chest and thought of what his next course of action should be. "I suppose I best get a lay of the land before anything else, figure out what this area looks like." He decided against climbing to the top of the tree since he was still precariously close to the guard towers and feared being seen popping out of the forest canopy. Instead, he climbed down from his perch and continued east, trying to put more distance between himself and the border.

After a few hours of travel, he felt confident he was more than far enough from the border and could safely climb up and get a better idea of his surroundings. But just when he was getting ready to stop, he noticed what looked like a clearing in the trees up ahead. He continued forward until reaching the edge of the treeline where he froze in stunned silence. He was looking at an open field, bright green sprinkled with tiny yellow flowers, which led to what looked like a small town. But what took him by surprise was what was directly behind the town. Mounds of earth that reached up into the clouds, with a skirt of green and capped with snow. "...what is this?" he whispered, looking at the wall of earth stretching farther than he could see in either direction. This was the first time Chronol had ever seen a mountain range and he was overwhelmed with its beauty. Leaning back against a tree, he marveled at the sight, still trying to process what towered before him.

"Quite the view, isn't it?" a voice asked. Chronol quickly darted away a few feet, immediately drawing his sword as he turned to face the source of the sound. There before him stood a man in simple clothes, a rope wrapped around his hand, going up over his shoulder and partially down his back. The other end was wrapped around the foot of a boar that laid limp at his back. His short black hair was stuck to his forehead with sweat. "Easy there, friend," he said soothingly, his light brown eyes staring at the glittering sword pointed at him. "I mean you no harm. I was just heading back home, didn't mean to startle you." Chronol stared at the man for a moment, looking him over, gauging his demeanor. He closed his eyes for a moment and let out a breath.

"I'm sorry," He replied, re-sheathing his sword. "I haven't been taken by surprise like that in quite some time. You move quite stealthily."

"My apologies," the man smiled, his eyes almost closing from his grin. "I'm accustomed to walking through these woods quietly so as not to disturb the wildlife. Makes it easier to hunt for dinner. I'm Daeril, by the way," he said, reaching his free hand forward.

"Nice to meet you, Daeril," Chronol replied, shaking his hand. "Do you live in that village there?"

"Yes," he nodded. "I take it you're not from around here?"

"You'd be correct," Chronol confirmed. "I'm just doing a bit of traveling, seeing the countryside, getting a better appreciation for the territory."

"Territory?" Daeril repeated as a look of suspicion crept across his face. Chronol noticed this but did his best to pretend nothing was wrong, trying to remain calm and casual. "I see..." he continued. "Well, I imagine you've seen some wonderful sights throughout the territory, I'm sure you have some interesting stories to tell."

"Not really," Chronol replied, trying to come up with a quick explanation. "A lot of the same thing, over and over. Grass, trees, an occasional town, the usual. It's been an uneventful trip thus far, nothing worth mentioning." He did his best to maintain his composure, hearing the tone change in the hunter's voice.

"Well, that's a shame," the man said, his feet shifting slightly. "I hear there are some interesting differences in the landscape between here and The Empire…"

Chronol's eyes grew wide hearing this, his grip slowly tightening around the handle of his sword. "I'm not sure what you mean…" he said cautiously, trying to gauge the danger of the situation.

"I'll ask you just once, stranger," Daeril said, slowly laying the boar on the ground, his other hand resting on the grip of his dagger. "Spy or refugee? Be careful of your response, I'm quite keen on seeing through deception."

Chronol could tell from the man's posture that the next words to come from his lips would decide the outcome of this encounter. He paused for a moment, then released the grip on his sword, raising his hands in a sign of surrender. "I'm a refugee," he answered. "The Kohtan army destroyed my home, I've come here to escape their influence. I give you my word, I mean you no harm."

The man stared at him for a moment, looking him over, reading his body language. He began to slowly pull his dagger from its sheath, staring intently at the stranger's eyes. Chronol made no movement whatsoever, remaining perfectly still despite seeing the weapon being drawn. The man paused, the blade almost drawn, and then resheathed it, seeming satisfied with what he had seen.

"Well," he spoke up, "in that case, welcome to the Kingdom of Caldor."

"Thank you…" Chronol said lowering his hands, relieved at the man's reaction. "I'm somewhat surprised you're so hospitable considering you know where I come from."

"Not all Kohtans are bad, I know better than to assume otherwise," he replied. "We're close to the Border of Kingdoms, you're not the first refugee to come this way. It's those controlling The Empire whose souls are tainted with darkness. Most of the people that come across the border are usually quite pleasant and kind, simply looking for an escape from the iron grip of The Empire. Occasionally we get a spy coming through, either posing as a refugee or simply trying to stay in the shadows. The Caldorian Knights do a fine job of finding them before they can cause too much trouble."

"I see," Chronol nodded. "Well that's good to hear. What about these refugees? Are they allowed residence in the kingdom or do they typically have to hide their existence?"

"Actually the kingdom is quite considerate towards their plight," Daeril explained. "Ever since the War of Kings, we Caldorians began to see the tyrannical rule that the Kohtans dominate their people with. We understand that their civilians aren't given many choices in life and are as much prisoners as they are residents. Thus, the kingdom is rather lenient when it comes to refugees taking residence within our borders. So long as they don't cause any trouble, they are free to find a home, find work and make a life here. I've never heard of any refugee being removed from the kingdom unless they were spies or bandits, and even then, the knights are more likely to toss them in the stockade than send them back over the border to cause more trouble in their hometowns."

"That's quite a gracious stance for them to take," the swordsman commented. "It seems your rulers are far more fair and kind than those across the border."

"We are truly blessed, I must say," Daeril agreed. "This is a beautiful land filled with peace and prosperity. Certainly, we have our share of thieves, bandits and the like; but the kingdom makes sure there are knights posted in every town that gets integrated into the kingdom, ensuring there is some form of law and protection in place to help them. They do a good job of keeping the peace and wrangling the ruffians."

They continued their conversation, losing track of time until the hunter's stomach began to rumble. "Goodness, it would appear the time has escaped us. It's been a pleasure talking with you but I should be heading to town to get this meat butchered and cooked. Do you have a place to stay for the evening?"

"Not really," Chronol replied, "but I'll make do. I'm growing accustomed to surviving on my own."

"Well, you could always come stay with me if you like," Daeril offered. "I have a spare room. It's mostly used to house my hunting tools and traps but there's a small bed in there if you'd like to use it. There's more than enough food here for two."

The thought of a hot meal and a warm bed out from under the stars and rain filled Chronol with a sense of excitement he hadn't felt in some time. But looking at the kind soul offering such hospitality, he was reminded of the bitter reality of his situation. Knowing that while what Daeril said was true, Chronol wasn't your ordinary refugee. He feared the lengths a Kohtan might go to in order to make sure their orders were fulfilled, how far they might travel, and who might get hurt in the crossfire. So despite wanting some relief from the wilds, he knew what needed to be done.

"I appreciate that," Chronol replied, "truly, I do. However, I think it's best if I stay on the move. There's much more land to be explored here it seems, and I should familiarize myself with this country. Nevertheless, you have my sincerest thanks."

"Very well," Daeril nodded, seeming to understand somewhat where the refugee was coming from. "I should let you get on your way then. Besides, this boar isn't going to prepare itself." They began to bid each other farewell when Chronol realized he had one more question for the gentlemen. "Oh, by the way. What is that?" he asked, pointing at the mounds of earth stretching as far as the eye could see.

"That?" Daeril smiled. "Why that's the Gordavian Mountains. I've heard most of the Empire is flatlands. Is it safe to assume this is your first time seeing mountains?"

"Yes," Chronol confirmed, "yes it is. They're quite beautiful, these moun...tens. Hm, what a curious word to use to describe them. How far do they reach?"

"Goodness," Daeril sighed, "quite the ways indeed. They stretch way up north to the Forests of Raehal and farther south than Torith. They nearly cut the kingdom in half."

"That sounds quite vast indeed," Chronol nodded. "Well I look forward to seeing more of their beauty throughout my travels. Thank you again for your kindness. It's a nice change of pace from the beginning of my journey."

"I imagine so," Daeril smiled. "Just know the offer remains, should you find yourself around here again. It's been a pleasure making your acquaintance. I wish you the best of luck and safety on your journey." With that, the two finally said their farewells and went their separate ways.

Despite the pleasant interaction with Daeril, Chronol remained vigilant about avoiding unnecessary contact with others. He would spend the next few months making his way north, little by little, keeping hidden as much as possible while observing the land and its people. He watched the soldiers that claimed to be there to serve and protect the people and was pleasantly surprised to see that this was more than just a claim. The Caldorian Knights were good men, faithful to their wards and did a wonderful job keeping the peace in the land. It felt so foreign from what he had experienced from the Kohtans, but at the same time it gave him a comforting feeling of home; reminding him of the Thoron soldiers he had served alongside. As the months turned to years, he continued to wander north, finding the forests that Daeril had mentioned, along with various other towns and villages along the way.

During his time in the north, he also stumbled upon the large Caldorian capital, Doruthan. An old but beautiful city, with an enormous tower in the center. Chronol snuck into the capital during the night to avoid too many questions. He did a little research and found that this massive tower was not the home of the king, but rather that of The White Weavers. Weavers, he discovered, were people with a special connection to magic that allowed them to not only see the wounds in a person's body, but to also heal those wounds. These Weavers were a group of very powerful healers who safe-guarded old texts of knowledge and secrets that they kept locked away in a vault in the tower. The king, on the other hand, stayed in a more modest keep just to the south of the tower. Had Chronol not asked about it from a local merchant, he would not have been able to tell it apart from a normal military barracks. Nothing ostentatious or gaudy or regal about it; just a normal, functional building. Chronol appreciated the humility as it reminded him of the elder of the Thorons. He kept his time in Doruthan short, since the city was more guarded and patrolled than other towns he'd visited thus far.

The years passed on while Chronol and Maksis made their way south along the other side of the Gordavian Mountains. Their travels were mostly pleasant, though on occasion they would stumble across people in need. A traveling merchant being robbed by thieves, a family trying to tend to wounds from an accident, a lost boy faint with thirst. Despite the long passage of time, Chronol's need to help people remained ingrained in him. Whenever he saw innocents suffering or being attacked, his instincts would take over and he would jump in to save them. He remained anonymous, simply rescuing the people and going on his way, but people always took notice of two things: his glowing green eyes, and the strange animal that accompanied him. Chronol realized wolfhounds were not a common sight in this kingdom, and with Maksis now fully grown and trained to assist him in combat, this made him stand out more than he liked. The small pup that had once seemed like a common dog was now much larger and more fierce looking. His black coat shifted to a mixture of dark red and black, with a stripe of white separating the two colors. His brown and silver eyes seemed almost haunting, and his stature grew akin to the largest of wolves. Nevertheless, the hound remained the same loyal and loving companion he had always been.

Chronol continued south until he reached a town called Torith. The name seemed familiar, like he had heard it somewhere before. Thinking back, he remembered Daeril mentioning it when they met years ago. The hunter stood out in his memory, being the first Caldorian Chronol had ever met. That memory prompted him to visit the town and see what it was like. He explored a little and found it to be a rather pleasant little farming town. Corn fields were seen all around, and the water for such crops could be traced back to a dam nearby. The people were kind and friendly, going out of their way to welcome him when they saw him looking around from a distance. He kept his hood drawn, attempting to keep his face hidden. When evening approached, a light rain began to come down. Chronol and Maksis made their way to one of the trees nearby to make camp for the night. Chronol climbed into the branches to sleep as he had grown accustomed to doing while his trusted companion slept at the base, no longer the tiny pup that could be carried into the branches like before. The storm grew stronger and more turbulent, the winds increasing along with the rain. Lightning crashing down woke Chronol from his slumber. The thunder seemed to quake and rumble forever, causing him to look out through the branches. What he saw made his heart skip a beat.

A wall of water came storming from the now broken dam like a tidal wave charging towards the little town. Before Chronol's feet could touch the ground, the water had already begun to destroy crops and buildings in its path. The swordsman charged forward, his wolfhound following alongside him. People outside the path of the wave could be heard screaming all around, shouting for their loved ones that were somewhere in the middle of this disaster. Without thinking, Chronol leapt through the air, grabbing hold of a tree just on the edge of the rushing water. People began to pop up from the water, one by one, grabbing a hold of whatever rooftop or post was nearby. He quickly dove into the water, swimming towards the person nearest to him. Grabbing the young woman and keeping her head above water, he made his way back towards land. He was met halfway by his trusted companion who paddled out to help. Chronol moved the woman to Maks's back and told him to take her to land. Maksis obediently paddled the woman to safety, the current pushing him a little further downriver. Once she was safe, the wolfhound would run back upriver and dive in again to continue helping. One after another, Chronol and Maksis saved the stranded villagers. Thanks to their efforts, over two dozen lives would see a new tomorrow. Chronol emerged from the water carrying the last of the survivors; a small child whose mother had nearly passed out watching in horror, hoping her child would be saved like the others.

While Chronol stood there in the rain, breathing heavily, the wind picked up and he reached to hold onto his hood, not realizing it had already fallen back while he was in the river. He slowly looked around at the villagers, his emerald eyes glowing in the darkness. "It's him..." one of the villagers said. "I've heard of this man... he's been saving people all over the kingdom. We are all in your debt, green-eyed guardian! Thank you for saving our families!"

Chronol looked down, averting his eyes from the crowd as more people began to cheer and applaud. He quickly returned the child to his mother. Pulling up his hood, he turned away and left the village behind. No matter how hard he tried to stay anonymous and keep a low profile, he could not stop people from talking about him; a mysterious man who saved strangers and disappeared without a word. And not giving his name only encouraged the people to find one for him. That name was The Green-Eyed Guardian.

9

The Youth

Chronol laid back on a rooftop gazing into the sky at the ocean of stars that glittered in the dark. The night air felt crisp and a cool breeze blew through the trees swaying branches that were illuminated by the moonlight His body grew heavier and his vision drifted to black as his eyelids began to close. Suddenly, an explosion woke him from his slumber. He quickly sat up to see the buildings around him ablaze and crumbling. Scrambling to his feet he stared at the destruction surrounding him. Looking to his left, he saw a familiar face standing near the edge. "...Rayz?" he whispered, "is that you? What happened?" Rayz looked back at Chronol, a small trickle of blood seeping from the corner of his mouth. The figure slouched forward slightly, then fell back with closed eyes, drifting off the edge of the building. "RAYZ, NO!" Chronol shouted, running forward and diving off the edge after his friend. He careened down, reaching out to grasp Rayz before he could hit the ground. Just before his hand could grasp his friend's limp body, he heard a thunderous *THUD*, and his eyes shot open to find his face planted into the grass.

"Ugh... my face..." he groaned, looking up from the grass and finding no buildings in sight. "Another dream..." he sighed, laying his face back into the grass. "I must've fallen from the tree." He laid still, staring at the palm of his hand. "It felt so real," he thought to himself. "Rayz... I'm so sorry..." Chronol whispered, a tear rolling across his face. He gripped a handful of grass, the blades popping and ripping in his hand. "I'm so... so sorry..." Maksis came over and laid beside his master, another tear falling from his eyes as he tried to go back to sleep. He had found some semblance of safety hiding in Caldor, but his mind was still haunted by the memory of those he'd lost. Year after year, he hoped they would fade away and leave him in peace, but time and time again his dreams turned to nightmares, reminding him again of the past he wished to forget. His only solace was in the name that had found him; The Green-Eyed Guardian. That fateful night in Torith a few years earlier had brought him face to face with more than just one or two saved travelers. That village had greatly spread the story of a guardian who roams the kingdom, thwarting evil and saving those in need. Attention and recognition he never wanted, but through the loneliness and mourning of his life, he found comfort in knowing that his continued existence at least served a purpose in saving others.

Over time, the kingdom grew and with that growth came rumors of a new group of bandits emerging from the Kohtan Empire. Marked by the crescent-shaped emblems hanging from their wrists, the Silver Moons were growing more notorious throughout the lands. Their attacks were swift and vicious, leaving only corpses and maimed survivors in their wake. The Caldorian knights did their best to stop these marauders, but it seemed whenever they focused military strength in one area, the bandits would simply move somewhere else. Chronol had heard reports that most of their activity took place in the northwest part of the kingdom and decided to start making his way in that direction.

After a few weeks of travel he came to the small town of Wilthen, a place he'd visited years ago, though only on the outskirts. It was a quaint little town west of the Gordavian Mountains. Chronol decided to make camp there for a day or two and attempt to gather new reports on the activities of the bandits he sought. The day after his arrival, he went into town and visited Bertrand's Tavern, a popular little establishment that seemed to draw in many travelers. The place wasn't much to look at from the outside except for the hand-carved sign out front. It had the tavern name as well as the likeness of a somewhat portly gentleman with a thick mustache and slicked-back hair. When he entered, Chronol was greeted with a pleasant melody being strummed on a guitar near the bar. There were a surprising number of people in the tavern considering the size of the town. Chronol began scanning the room, looking for anyone who seemed particularly friendly or talkative that might easily share news from abroad. During his search he spotted a man who looked suspiciously like the figure carved into the sign, standing behind the counter. Deciding to blend in, he headed over to the barkeep to order a drink.

"You must be the famous Bertrand, I presume?" Chronol asked, keeping his hood pulled down to hide his eyes.

"Why, yes, I am, stranger," the gentleman nodded. "It's a pleasure to make your acquaintance. I am Bertrand Felthistle, owner and operator of this fine establishment. To whom do I have the honor of addressing?"

"Oh, no one of any import, I assure you," Chronol responded. "Just a wanderer passing through, looking for a drink and a good story," he explained, sliding a gold coin across the bar. "I don't suppose I could trouble you for a glass of water?"

"Yes... that's quite doable," Bertrand responded, looking curiously at the hooded figure before him. "I'll have that right up for you." The barkeep quickly filled a glass and handed it to the swordsman, who nodded appreciatively and began to drink, careful not to tilt his head back.

"That's fine water indeed," Chronol commented with a sigh. "Now then, I don't suppose you've had any travelers passing through here with stories of the goings on around the kingdom, have you? I hoped I might be able to catch up on any news as of late."

"Well... there was a gentleman earlier who said he was a traveling merchant and had just arrived in town," the barkeep replied. "I do believe he's still sitting there in the corner." He pointed towards a table not far from the entrance to the tavern.

"Why, thank you, sir," Chronol responded. "I very much appreciate it. If you'll excuse me." He stood up and headed towards the merchant. Along the way, three new patrons entered the tavern, brushing past Chronol and his wolfhound on their way to the bar. They wore garbs of black cloth and brown leather, their hair shoulder-length and raven dark. Something about them caused him to pause for a moment before continuing towards the merchant; however, before he could introduce himself, the music was interrupted by a crash of discordant notes. Chronol turned towards the sound and saw pieces of guitar flying through the air. One of the new patrons had smashed the instrument over the head of the musician.

"Nobody move!" one of the ruffians shouted as they began drawing their blades.

"Everyone just stay calm, remain seated, and prepare any valuables you might have. We'll be making our way around the room momentarily to relieve you of any burdensome items that might be weighing down your person," another thug explained. "Oh, and if you find yourself feeling heroic, might I discourage you with the following…" he said, quickly piercing the heart of the musician with his sword. People gasped at the sight. When he withdrew his blade, the man's body slowly fell to the tavern floor. "So, please, take that into consideration before deciding to do something stupid," he grinned.

Chronol raised his hands in a sign of surrender as he approached the bandits. "Ah ah ah!" one of them called out after seeing him approach. "What did I say about stupid heroics?"

"I'm not a hero…" Chronol whispered. The bandit kept his eyes trained on the approaching stranger while one of the others began demanding all of the coin behind the bar.

"Very well, just stupid then?" the apparent leader of the bandits asked, raising his sword. A crescent shaped charm dangled from his wrist. "Or are you so anxious to relinquish your belongings that you thought you'd walk to the front of the line and save us some time?" he smirked.

"Not quite…" Chronol responded. In an instant the thief found himself face to face with the approaching stranger, a gap of 10 feet closed in the blink of an eye. Before he could process what was happening, the sound of cracking bones echoed into his ears. He looked down to find his sword clattering to the ground, his hand twisted and broken in several different places. The man screamed out in pain as he clutched his mangled hand and fell to his knees. The other two turned around, unsure of what had just happened. One of them lunged at Chronol with his blade in hand, only to find it parried by a silver sword. The other bandit joined the fray and the two of them began attacking him wildly. One after another, each strike was dodged or deflected. A spatter of blood hit the floor when Chronol stabbed the sword hand of one bandit, forcing him to drop his blade. The third hesitated, seeing what had happened to his companion, and no sooner did he pause that he felt the wind escape his lungs. Chronol had planted his boot in the man's chest, breaking some of his ribs. As quickly as the fight began, it was over. Each bandit lay disarmed and writhing in pain on the floor. The patrons of the establishment were frozen in stunned silence, looks of disbelief on their faces. Chronol sheathed his sword and walked up to the first bandit he had dealt with. He grabbed the man by his collar and lifted him up off the ground, bringing him face to face with the one who had destroyed his hand.

"Look at me…" Chronol demanded. "What do you see?" Shakily, the bandit looked into his captors' face and saw that the hood of the mysterious swordsman had slid back, revealing eyes that glowed like fiery emeralds.

"That… that's not… that's not possible…" he whimpered. "You're…"

"Yes," Chronol interrupted. "That's right. You know who I am."

"But… they're just stories…" the bandit whined. "They can't be real… YOU can't be real…"

"Unfortunately for you, I am…" Chronol growled. "Look into these eyes and know. See for yourself exactly what awaits you and your ilk if you continue to harass these lands. This kingdom and her people are protected by The Green-Eyed Guardian. Let your superiors know that if they mean to do harm in these lands, they do so at their own peril. I will hunt down and find each and every one of you until not a single man is left that can hold a sword. You make them understand, Caldor is OFF LIMITS. Go back to the empire and do not return. This is your only warning…" Chronol released the bandit, who began crying and shaking on the floor. Adjusting his hood back into place, he glanced around at the shocked patrons. "I apologize for the disturbance," he said, walking towards the door. "Someone should fetch the Knights so they can collect these bandits." As he exited the tavern with Maksis by his side, a voice could be heard whispering from amongst the people inside, saying, "That was him…"

Chronol hurried out of town before he could draw further attention, his purpose of sending a message now fulfilled. It was the first time in a decade that he had actually used the moniker the people had given him, and he hoped it would be enough to dissuade the marauders from future attacks. Unfortunately, over the passing months he discovered that his message was indeed received, though the response was not what he hoped for. It seemed that the Silver Moon leaders felt a challenge was issued and rather than backing down, they proceeded to increase their brazen attacks and robberies. Chronol found himself racing from town to town trying to stop them and being met with the harsh reality that he couldn't be in all places at once. Each time he encountered one of their groups, he did his best to inflict injuries that would prevent them from being able to fight again in the future. Years passed this way and the Silver Moons seemed to gain new recruits as quickly as he disabled them.

Eventually, Chronol started finding the rumors of Silver Moon activity to be traps set up by the bandits themselves, whispered about just to lure him in. It appeared he had disrupted their business enough that they decided to take the fight directly to him. This actually worked out in his favor, allowing him to take on and cripple more of them at a time without having to search as hard. This plan of theirs eventually backfired, and a kind of unspoken truce came about. The Silver Moons stuck to robbing and killing stray travelers on the roads, leaving the towns and villages of Caldor alone. While it wasn't a complete surrender and evacuation from the kingdom, Chronol couldn't help but feel like it was at least a partial win now that the towns and villages were safe again.

Sitting by a lake washing his face, he pondered on the years of warring with the gang. He looked down at his reflection and came to a realization. "All these years of running, wandering, rescuing, warring…" he thought. "Why do I still look the same? Nothing's changed. It's like looking in a mirror from well over a decade ago." He stared into the water, seeing the visage of a young man looking back at him with piercing green eyes. "I thought it was just the eyes that changed. I mean, sure I seem a little stronger and faster than before, but this is something different. I don't know what's happening to me…" He looked over to his four-legged companion who stared back with brown and silver eyes. "Do I look any older to you?" he asked. Maksis tilted his head to the side as he looked back at his master. "Yeah… I didn't think so."

His life of wandering, saving innocents, and making war on a gang of bandits kept Chronol too occupied to notice the strange happenings with his body. He started to keep an eye on his appearance more intently as time passed, but while the kingdom expanded, and camps became villages, and villages became towns, and the seasons passed, the one thing that seemed frozen in time was his age. The passage of time seemed faster and faster to him. Weeks felt like days, years like months. It was like he was moving through life on fast forward, each event in his travels just a fleeting moment that was here one second and gone the next.

Chronol eventually returned to that little town, nestled in the shadow of the Gordavian Mountains, where he met his first Caldorian. He was careful not to be noticed, keeping to the trees and just watching from afar. After a few days, he saw a middle-aged man heading towards the woods with a young boy. They had bows and hunting knives and a length of rope. He watched the pair closely from his perch in a nearby tree, and as they passed below him his eyes widened. The man passing by was, in fact, Daeril, the one he came looking for. The hunter's short, black hair was now longer and sprinkled with grey. The young boy beside him looked to be roughly ten or eleven years old and bore a striking resemblance to Daeril. The two made their way into the woods, clearly out for an afternoon hunt, unaware they were being watched.

This was the confirmation Chronol wanted to see with his own eyes. His mind had started playing tricks on him, making him think his concept of time had grown warped in his solitude. His subconscious tried to make sense of a phenomenon that had no plausible explanation. However, seeing Daeril older and with apparently an adolescent son, it confirmed what Chronol always suspected to be true. It wasn't just his perception of time that changed, but something inside him. Whatever happened, he wanted answers. This was something unlike anything he'd ever heard of before. He knew better than to return to the empire to seek the answers, so he decided it was time to search Caldor. It would mean interacting with people more, which still worried him, but he needed to understand what was happening to him and why. His wandering now became a journey to find the truth.

10

The Scholar

Candlelight glowed across an old wooden table, illuminating a weathered open book. A mug of water reflected a glimmer of light as a hand turned a page. Glowing green eyes peered from behind a hood, staring down at the text in front of them. The book's content seemed to be about uncommon diseases and inherited traits. Page after page, Chronol continued through the book, sitting in the corner of a dimly lit room. A creak of wood could be heard across the room as an older gentleman shifted in his chair. Eventually the swordsman finished reading the book, closing the cover and sighing gently. "Ugh… nothing here," he thought to himself. "I guess it was worth a shot." Standing up from his seat, he put the book back on a nearby shelf and walked over to the older man. "Thank you, sir. Here's your coin," he said sliding a gold coin across the counter.

"Thank you, young man," the gentleman responded. "You've certainly been spending a lot of time reading through the books here. Should I expect you again tomorrow around the same time?"

"No, I think I've exhausted what's here," Chronol answered. "It may be time to move on and search elsewhere."

"My apologies, son," said the man. "I don't have a whole lot of medical books here. They're a little harder to come by this far from the capital. Perhaps you'll have better luck further north."

"Yes," Chronol nodded, "I think I may just do that. Thank you again for your time and hospitality. I wish you and your library well. Good day." He bowed slightly and began walking to the door.

"Thank you, sir," the gentleman smiled. "May your journey be a safe one."

Chronol had spent the better part of a month searching through whatever medical books he could get his hands on in Kestel, a small town in the southwest of Caldor. He was hoping he'd find some reference to the things happening to his body; anything that would explain his glowing eyes, extended youth, and his improved strength and speed. Unfortunately, their selection was limited and provided no answers. With this location fully searched, he decided to head north, hoping a town closer to the capital might have what he sought.

He made his way towards Doruthan, keeping closer to the mountains as this area of the kingdom was uncomfortably close to the border. In this way, he was able to quietly make his way across the countryside to the next town unnoticed. Again, he searched, but to no avail. Nothing in their library or bookstore seemed to have any relevant information. He moved on from one town or village to the next, the months turning to years. Each time he found a new location to search, he would bury himself in books, study, and research. Each time, hopeful this might be the location that gives him some answers, and each time walking away disappointed and a little more discouraged. In the town of Comen, he met an old man well-studied in a variety of subjects from math to medicine to philosophy. The gentleman was friendly and took an interest in Chronol's desire to research medicine and genetics. He allowed the Thoron to pick his brain and together they came to the conclusion that the only plausible explanation was magic, and the only ones known to manipulate a person's health with magic were the Weavers. Chronol was given a renewed sense of hope, having a new lead to pursue. He thanked the man for his sage wisdom and insight and continued on with his investigation, this time making a point of hunting for any documents related to or written by Weavers.

Making his way around the mountains, part of him knew where he should be looking, but he feared being discovered and what reaction people might have to his condition. He continued to visit the smaller towns, finding a few books about Weavers and healing, but nothing that even remotely seemed to reference what was happening to him. Along the way, he encountered the occasional person in need, and he would help them as he always did. But unlike before, his mind remained focused on finding answers rather than his previous task of wandering aimlessly.

After exhausting his safest options, he had two places left he hadn't really searched yet. One, for fear of recognition, and the other for fear of confinement. He was confronted with a choice: Head to Torith, the place where he was most likely to be recognized, or head to Doruthan, and risk being noticed by the increased security. Torith had since recovered and grown much larger than before. The broken dam, rather than be repaired, had become a port which allowed supplies to be shipped down from Clarin, a city in the North near the capital. As such, they would certainly have more resources than before, however, they could still recognize him and he did not want the attention. His worry about being found in Doruthan was simply because people usually feared the unknown. He didn't know if they would be accepting or not of his unique condition. Would they allow him to wander around the capital researching or would they attempt to detain him for study? He sat by the campfire, running his fingers through Maksis' coat, pondering his next move. "What do you think, boy?" he asked. "North or south?" Maks sat for a moment, staring at his master, then scratched behind his ear and let out a howl to the moon. "You make a convincing argument," Chronol sighed. "Fine, if it's information on Weavers we seek, then to their home we shall go. In the morning... we make for Doruthan."

And so they did, heading north for the capital he had been trying to avoid. Along the way, he thought back to his first visit into the capital. He remembered the gap in security during the night shift and how he was able to slip into town unnoticed after dark. This would be the way he would attempt to regain entry. When finally arriving at Doruthan he looked for the gap in security and, with careful precision, managed to enter the city again without being seen. With phase one complete, he now needed to figure out where to find information and if there was any way to gain access to the Weaver's Tower.

The following day he asked around and found out that there were apparently several libraries in this city, which gave him plenty of locations to conduct his research. The tower, unfortunately, was an entirely different story. "The Archive," as it was called, was where the White Weavers lived, trained, studied, and most importantly, kept certain artifacts under lock and key in a place they called The Vault. Because of this, White Weavers constantly guarded the entry to the tower, which was open only to the Weavers and the king's guard. Chronol quickly realized he wouldn't be getting inside that location without a fight, and that was something he wouldn't do. So instead, he settled on searching the libraries, hoping to finally find some answers. There was plenty of information on weavers in general, as well as the faction that call themselves The White Weavers, but he found nothing in their history indicating that they have any capability to do what seems to have been done to him. After nearly two months of hiding and searching, he once again hit another wall.

Frustrated, Chronol left Doruthan and headed south, tired of not finding any answers. He decided to make a trek into the Gordavian Mountains to clear his head and get away from civilization for a time. From its snow-covered peaks he could see the whole kingdom, including the white shores of Clarin, the dense, green forests of Raehal and even as far as the Border of Kingdoms. While up there, he spent time clearing his mind and playing with his wolfhound, attempting to feel normal, if only for a passing moment. Gradually, he unwound enough to clear his mind, and the aggravation of searching for years with no answers began to fade away. One day, while playing in the icy snow with Maks, he looked into a smooth, shimmering piece of ice and saw the reflection of his eyes glowing back at him. His desire for answers began to stir up again, and he decided with all the time that had passed perhaps it was safe to return to Torith and see what he might find there.

He began traveling down the other side of the mountains, and along the way he spotted something. Chronol looked down, seeing steel armor glimmer and crested banners wave in the small clearing at the foot of the mountains. It was an encampment of patrolling Caldorian knights. Their tents were clearly marked with the crest of the kingdom. Some knights were circled around the campfire where a freshly caught boar roasted over the flames, filling the air with the aroma of cooked meat. They silently observed Chronol's descent.

"Greetings, traveler," a young knight said as Chronol finally drew near, "how fares your journey?"

"It continues, Captain. It seems like I've been travelling forever," said Chronol.

"Your journey sounds like a long one. Where are you headed?" asked the captain.

"I'm just heading to Torith to visit an old friend," he responded, hoping the knight wouldn't pry further.

"I see. Very well, I bid you and your four-legged companion safe travels," the captain smiled.

Chronol bid him farewell and headed through the camp until he heard a shrill sound behind him. He turned around to find a griffon landing in the encampment. The knights swiftly drew their weapons, "Griffon! Into formation men, quickly!" shouted the captain. The golden beast towered over the knights, the wind from its powerful wings blowing over some of their tents. The knights surrounded the griffon, trying their best to block its attacks with their shields. The animal turned and whipped two of the knights to the ground with its long tail. Front foot swinging forward, talons sank into the metal of the captain's shield, tearing it from his hands. He stood there in fear, his sword raised trying to fend off the griffon. It reared back, preparing to strike him down. He closed his eyes, ready for the attack, but nothing happened. When he opened his eyes he saw the swordsman's back in front of him. Silver sword at the ready and shield in hand, he stood there between the soldier and the winged creature. The captain looked up to see the beast flailing as Maksis stood on its back, biting and tearing at one of its wings.

"Order your men back, Captain!" Chronol shouted, "We'll handle the griffon, you tend to the wounded!"

The captain quickly ordered his men to fall back to a safer position, but remained behind Chronol. "I will not allow you to fight this beast alone!" he shouted.

"Fine," Chronol responded, "but you stay back and wait until I tell you there's an opening." The captain agreed as he picked up another shield.

Chronol lunged forward, slashing one of the legs of the beast and made his way around to the griffon's side. The captain called out to Chronol, warning him to watch out for the wing. "Not a problem," Chronol said, pointing at the creature's back. The captain realized the griffon's wing was useless thanks to the damage done by Maksis, who had moved on to bite and tear at the other wing. The beast became more desperate as it found itself unable to fly and began lashing out violently. It swung at Chronol who dodged to the side, deflecting some of the strike upwards with his shield. He then followed up his defense by stabbing the back of the griffon's leg, which brought out another screech from the beast. It turned toward Chronol, the rage in its eyes building, its body poised to strike.

"Prepare yourself, Captain," Chronol called out, "the back left leg on my command!" The soldier prepared himself, his blade at the ready. Chronol clashed his sword against his shield, shouting at the griffon. The beast lashed out, biting at him. He slid under its belly and shouted "Now!" The captain leapt forward, stabbing his sword into the creature's back left leg as Chronol stabbed up into its left shoulder. It cried out, falling on its side, still lashing out with its right limbs. "Careful!" the captain shouted, "It's still fighting back!" Suddenly, the edge of a silver blade came up out of the griffon's right shoulder. The arm shook, then stopped moving. Chronol got up from beneath the beast, unscathed, standing over its neck. "I'm sorry," he said, "let me end this suffering." He placed his boot on the griffon's neck to hold it still. Its once enraged eyes were now full of pain and fear. He pierced the head with his sword and finally it remained still and ceased crying. He knelt down beside it, stroking the beast's head, the golden brown feathers stained red with blood.

"Poor creature, I didn't want to hurt you. But I couldn't very well let you kill these men over a boar now, could I?" Maksis came and licked the griffon's face. Chronol ran his fingers through the wolfhound's brown and black coat, "I know Maks, you're sorry, too."

The captain walked over to Chronol, with a look of utter amazement. "Sir, you were incredible!" he exclaimed. "You and your four-legged companion are a force to be reckoned with. You must come back with our unit to Doruthan so we can properly reward your bravery."

Chronol stood up, wiping his blade and putting his sword and shield away.

"That won't be necessary," he said, "I'm just glad you and your men are alright. If you wish to reward me, try to be more careful in the future. It's dangerous roasting a boar so close to the mountains."

The captain pleaded with Chronol to reconsider, but to no avail. "I don't recognize that crest. May I at least know the name of the man who saved us?" he asked.

"I'm unimportant, just a wandering traveler," the Thoron responded.

"You know, taking into account the hidden identity and the wolfhound, I would be inclined to think you were the Green-Eyed Guardian considering how you miraculously saved us just now. But you're clearly only a few years older than I. There's no way you could be that old legend," he smiled.

Chronol looked up, grinning, his eyes shining through the shade of his hood, "Yes, I suppose I am a bit too young to be him." The captain was speechless, a look of shock on his face as he saw the swordsman's eyes glowing that famed green. Chronol patted him on the shoulder and walked away, bidding farewell to the rest of the soldiers as he left.

The captain returned to the rest of his men, "It's true…" he said, "it's all true…" They asked him what he was talking about. "The legends, the stories, all of it. He really does exist." His men looked on in confusion, still unsure of what he was talking about. They asked who the traveler was, and he responded, "Gentlemen, we were just saved by the Green-Eyed Guardian…" Some of them believed what the captain said, while others simply labeled the man a wanderer; however, they would all remember that day for the rest of their lives.

Chronol continued to walk onward, the smile fading from his face. "Why did I do that?" he thought to himself. "What if they had tried to arrest or detain me? I couldn't bring myself to harm them. That was an unnecessary risk." He couldn't understand why, but something in him seemed to be breaking. It was as if the fear of being seen was starting to drift away. But despite his reckless display, he kept reminding himself it was safer for everyone if he remained hidden and anonymous.

"But you're clearly only a few years older than I. There's no way you could be that old legend." Those words continued to echo in his mind. "I need answers," he thought. "Please, let there be answers in Torith."

Continuing south, he eventually found his way to the little town he had saved decades ago. He was surprised to find it had grown so much. His last memory of this place was that of a small and partially flooded village, drenched in rain and lit with lightning. Now, he found himself looking at a proper town. The homes were rebuilt and updated, the farmlands had regrown, and a port now stood in place of the dam. A ship could be seen in the harbor, unloading supplies. It warmed his heart to see this place recovering so well. He headed into town, looking to find a library or bookstore of some sort. What he found, however, left him speechless. A stone-carved figure stood in the center of town. Chronol immediately recognized the figure on display to be himself. The same armor, the same cloak, it was clearly him. The details of the face were somewhat vague, which he was thankful for, but to his surprise the eyes were emeralds, glittering in the sunlight. A plaque with an inscription was wrapped around the base of the statue. "Erected in memory of those we lost in the flood, and in honor of the one who saved so many of our lives that day. Blessed be The Green-Eyed Guardian." Aside from the message, the remainder of the plaque had a list of names under the heading "Lost to the Storm" and another list of names under "Saved by our Hero."

Chronol did his best to keep his emotions in check, but he couldn't help feeling a mixture of pride and sadness. He was happy so many had survived and were thankful for his help, but also mourned the loss of the ones he couldn't save. Worried someone might see him next to the statue, he quickly left the town center. He walked through the town, eventually finding a library and searching their books for any answers or clues, but once again found nothing of use. With no idea what to do next and feeling quite defeated, Chronol wandered out to the docks and sat on the pier looking into the water. Closing his eyes and thinking back to all the years of searching and hoping, he wondered if it was all for nothing.

"I'm telling you, Gellan, that land mass wasn't there before," a man's voice said. Chronol slowly pulled himself back to the present and looked around, spotting a couple sailors unloading some crates onto the pier.

"You're daft in the head," the other man replied. "Land doesn't just spring up out of the ocean. That was probably just an island we hadn't seen before."

"Really?" the first sailor continued. "You think after years of making that trip over and over, that we missed an island THAT big? Are you sure I'm the one that's daft?"

"Well," Gellan answered, "the ocean is a big place. It's perfectly possible we've missed an island here and there. It's not as if we're just now discovering a whole new continent, though."

11

The Sailor

The sun began to set on the horizon covering the countryside in an orange glow. Green hills tinted by the dusk light surrounded the area, grass swaying in the gentle breeze. The sound of creaking wood echoed across the field. A small group of travelers led their cart down a path that was ground to dirt from decades of use. As the family continued down the peaceful road, a handful of figures clad in dark clothes stepped out from the brush along the path. The man steering the cart pulled back on the reins, slowing the cart to a stop when the group gathered in front of him.

"Well, good evening sir," one of the men in black called out. "How goes your travels this fine day?"

"Peacefully," the gentleman on the cart responded. "We're just making our way down to the next town."

"Well, that's just wonderful," said the man, smiling. "Im glad your journey hasn't been fraught with too much danger, yet."

"Yes…" the man on the cart murmured, trying to hide a look of suspicion. The woman beside him squeezed his arm a little tighter and stared silently at the men who had stopped them. "Is there something I can do for you?" the gentleman asked.

"Oh, no," the smiling man answered, "actually it's I who wishes to do something for you. You see, there's been some new taxes issued as of late. We're just going around making sure everyone is made aware and given the opportunity to square away any debt they might unknowingly have with the kingdom." As he continued his explanation, the men behind him began to slowly fan out, surrounding the cart.

"We want no trouble, gentlemen," the traveler answered, slowly moving his arm to guard the woman beside him. "We're simply trying to pass through."

"Well, you see," the dark clothed man continued, "that's the issue. You're traveling down the king's highway, but unfortunately there's been a new tax levied which requires you to pay to use said highway. Tell me, have you paid your traveler's tax for using this road? I haven't received any reports of people matching your description paying their travel tax yet."

"I've heard of no such tax," the traveler responded, gripping the reins tighter as he tried to keep track of the men surrounding them. The woman's grasp around his arm started to tremble.

"Yes, well it's very new," the other man explained. "We'll have to collect said taxes before you're able to move on. Plus a penalty fee for using the road without paying ahead of time. Also there's the collector's fee for making us intercept you on the road instead of paying in the capital…" The man went on listing fee after fee, each one sounding more made up than the last. "Look, just give us all of your gold and we'll call it even. Sound fair?"

"It most certainly does not," the traveler responded, seeing these men were clearly thieves. "I will do no such thing, now please get out of our way. I have a family that I need to take care of and I cannot afford to be swindled by highway robbers trying to make an easy gold by preying on traveling families. You all should be ashamed of yourselves."

"What's that?" the leader of the bandits asked. "What did you call us?" He approached the cart, drawing a sword from his belt. "I think you should choose your words more carefully when addressing people who hold your life in their hands," he warned, pointing his sword towards the woman, a crescent shaped charm hanging from his wrist. "…and the lives of your dear family."

"No, please!" he begged, attempting to put himself between the blade and his wife. "I meant no disrespect. Please, there's no need to threaten them, they have nothing to do with it."

"My, how quickly your tune has changed," the thief laughed loudly. "I need only snap my fingers and you would watch your entire family slain before you. Perhaps you should keep that in mind when addressing a Silver Moon. We are NOT to be trifled with." While the bandit explained how trapped the travelers truly were, a pair of silhouettes could be seen walking up the road.

"Hey, Goen," the thief near the back of the wagon called out, "it looks like we got another. This one's on foot."

"Well," the bandit leader replied, "detain our new friend and explain to him his situation." As the silhouettes came into view, it was that of a man and what looked like a large wolf.

The bandit smiled and approached them, calling out. "Hey! You! I'm gonna have to stop you here for a moment. Capital business and all that." The man and his companion continued to approach, walking up to the thief that confronted them. "There we are. Now then, this is the king's highway, you need to pay your taxes for using it, blah blah blah, give us all your gold or else we'll have to penalize you." The bandit drew a dark, battle-worn sword from his belt and brought it up to the man's chin. "Oh, and you won't like the penalty for not paying." Looking the traveler over, he noticed the beautiful sword at his side. "Ooo, and how about that shiny sword of yours as well. You know, a little extra for gratuity," he smiled, reaching for the handle. In a brief flash of light, the bandit found his blade parried to the ground, and a glimmering silver sword pressed gently against his throat.

"Oh, you mean THIS sword?" Chronol responded. The thief remained motionless, his eyes darting around trying to comprehend what just happened. Chronol reached forward and took the man's hand, turning it to reveal the charm on his wrist. "I figured as much. I would've thought you boys learned your lesson by now. You know Caldor is off limits. You know you can't attack the villages here without incurring my ire. Why don't you just leave this kingdom and go back to the empire already."

"Listen, stranger," the disarmed thief replied, "I don't know who you are but you need to back off before my allies tear you apart." As he spoke, the other bandits, noticing there was an altercation happening with the new traveler, immediately began to approach the pair. "See, now you've done it."

The young bandit suddenly cried out in pain as his wrist made a loud cracking sound. "The only thing I've done is break your wrist," Chronol responded. "You should know your place, this conflict has gone on longer than you've been alive." He looked to the other thieves surrounding him and called out. "I have no interest in crippling all of you. Which one of you is the leader?"

"Why, that'd be me, my suicidal friend," Goen smiled, stepping forward. "Now then, what in magic's name would make you think it was a good idea to break my boy's wrist here, hm? Now I have to charge you extra for damages to…" before he could finish his sentence the swordsman seemed to appear out of nowhere, ending up inches away from the man, the tip of his hood almost touching Goen's nose.

"We have an agreement," Chronol whispered softly. "You leave the people of this land alone, I don't remove your limbs. Now, I'm not stupid enough to think that you never poke your heads out of the ground from time to time to hold up the occasional traveler, but if you think I'll let it happen right in front of me, you've got another thing coming." A slow, deep growl began to emanate from the black and red wolfhound beside him. "Now then," he said, lifting his head towards Goen, "perhaps you'll have the good sense to disarm your men for me and excuse yourselves." Chronol's piercing green eyes flared from under his hood. The bandit just stared in disbelief, unable to look away.

"But… but you're just a nursery rhyme… something they tell us to keep us to the code…" Goen whispered, barely able to speak. "You're not… you…" Chronol just shook his head slowly, side to side.

"Do I look like a bedtime story to you?" he growled.

Trembling, the bandit leader slowly put down his sword and looked to his group. "Everyone, drop your weapons… now…" he called out. They looked at each other, confused as to what could have happened that would prompt such an uncharacteristic order. "I SAID DROP THEM!" he shouted, seeing their hesitation. The robbers dropped their weapons one by one, some pulling secondary daggers from their belts or boots. "May… may we please leave, sir?"

"Go…" Chronol answered, "and pray we don't meet again. I will be far less lenient next time…" The man slowly stepped back and gestured for the rest of his men to follow.

"We're moving out, let's go," Goen called out to his group. One by one, they filed out, disappearing back into the brush. Chronol let out a sigh as he shook his head.

"Ugh, when will they learn," he groaned. "Their lives could be so much more." Maksis remained vigilant, staring into the brush, growling softly until his master stroked the hound's ears back. "It's fine, boy. They're gone." Maks began to wag his tail slowly, returning to his normal friendly demeanor. The duo continued down the road, passing by the travelers who were still sitting in their wagon, collecting themselves after the close call.

"Sir," the man called out while consoling his wife. "I can't thank you enough. We are forever indebted to you."

"You owe me nothing," Chronol responded, "I'm glad your family is alright."

"That fact is thanks to you. But… I have to ask," the traveler continued. "Who are you? Are you some great general or lord to exude such power with only words? You must be someone of great import."

"I'm no one of consequence," Chronol replied, "just a traveler passing through. Perhaps they simply had a change of heart. Regardless, I should be going. Safe travels to you and your family." Bidding them farewell, he continued down the road.

"Oh, um, alright," the man called out. "Thank you again!" He looked at his wife who had stopped crying. She was watching the man and his wolfhound walking away.

"Who was that man, I wonder," she sniffled.

Chronol had given up on finding answers since his last failure in Torith. He'd since gone back to just wandering, trying to keep his mind off of the fact that he had spent the better part of two decades searching and gotten no closer to knowing the truth. He made his way east until he found himself at the port city of Clarin.

The city had grown greatly over the years, but still remained a relatively relaxed location in terms of security and prying eyes. Chronol walked into town and headed to the Salty Seahorse, a small tavern by the docks. He ordered a drink and, by force of habit, took a seat in a darker corner, Maks curling up in the shadow behind him. He sat back and closed his eyes, listening to the sounds of the tide muffled through the walls. Relaxing, he could hear conversations from the different tables of patrons around him. Some discussed life on the open sea, others about a recent change in the weather. One group, however, began discussing The Risen Continent. Chronol remembered the first time he had heard about that land, years ago in Torith. Since then it had been confirmed that what was first thought to be a large island, was in fact an entire continent. The Caldorian Knights had restricted access to it while they surveyed the land, investigating the area for dangers. They also established a port city, in addition to a centralized military camp from which to maintain order. The merchants conversing were excited that the Caldorian government had finally opened the route to the public, allowing civilians to travel there.

"Hmm... a new land," Chronol thought to himself. "Something new would be a nice change of pace." Thankfully, living off the land allowed him to save most of his gold, giving him enough money to get a ticket and board one of the ships heading for The Risen Continent. The charter vessel set sail and headed northeast. Several weeks later they arrived in a shabby skeleton of a port town. So new, in fact, that it had only recently been given a name; Tesatul. It was the only port on this continent thus far. The ship made its way into the docks and tied off, allowing its passengers to disembark. Chronol was happy to be back on dry land and quickly began exploring the town. It was still too soon for there to be anything of real value to him, such as a library, but it was a new place, nonetheless. After spending a little time in Tesatul, he decided to venture out into the wilds and see for himself what this land was like.

Outside of town there was nothing but green wilderness as far as the eye could see. These lands were largely untouched thus far and it was an interesting change from the more populated lands of the The Old Continent. Little by little, he made his way around, seeing if there were any unique areas that were worth exploring. One thing he did notice was an increase in danger from wildlife due to the lack of settled areas. Beasts roamed almost everywhere, causing him to have to defend himself quite often. He searched on, looking for any communities that might have already been established, but to no avail. Secretly, he had hoped to find a whole new group of people here that already inhabited this land, a group that might be more well versed in whatever was happening to him. Unfortunately, despite searching for many years, he found no indigineous towns or villages on this continent and eventually gave up. He quit searching for people, quit searching for answers, and quit searching for an explanation. The only thing left to do was to simply accept that this was his life now, that he was different and there was nothing he could do to change or understand it. It seemed that the only thing that was visibly changed about his appearance was his eyes and lack of aging, so he decided it was no longer worth searching for. After more than twenty years of trying to find an answer that wasn't out there, he was ready to resign to the fact that this was just the way things would be.

On the other hand, he did find himself busier here than he had been in quite some time in The Old Continent. While the southern continent has a well established series of barracks and patrols and soldiers a plenty, this new land was quite dangerous. People began pouring in from the old continent; some searching for adventure, others for a new life, others for riches. The vast majority of them didn't stay in Tesatul, but instead ventured off to establish new towns and villages across the country. This meant a lot of attacks from wild animals while the local ecosystem adapted to the presence of new inhabitants. Chronol found himself keeping an eye on a lot of travelers during these times. He also found himself having to deal with more bandit activity, as groups of them had begun coming to the new country hidden amongst the civilians. They sought to take advantage of a land that lacked the military supervision to keep everyone well guarded. He spent a good deal of his time protecting travelers and merchants, watching over new settlements, keeping an eye from the shadows to make sure neither bandit nor beast interfered with the lives of these innocents.

With so much to keep him occupied, Chronol focused on his work and let it consume him. Gradually, over the years, he started to find some semblance of peace by accepting that the answers didn't matter anymore. What mattered was that he was different, and he could either let that fact control his life, or he could control that new facet of his being and use it. He chose the latter, realizing that this world needed a guardian. Seeing the lack of change in appearance as the decades accumulated, he realized few would be more qualified to take on that responsibility than him. This would be his purpose, his mission; to safeguard this land and protect those in it when the ones in power weren't able. And so, he stood watch over The Risen Continent while the decades continued to pass by.

He saw a shabby dock grow and change. Merchants and craftsmen joined the building effort until the once barely standing dock grew into a port city like its counterpart on The Old Continent. The handful of stalls selling fish and other products expanded into a full blown market square. The rickety dock barely able to handle two boats multiplied ten-fold, able to accept ships of every size. The population grew as a residential district was established, with new homes being built every day. The handful of guards expanded into a proper military barracks, with soldiers to inspect people and shipments coming into port, trying to maintain a semblance of order in this new world.

He watched wandering travelers establish camps further and further north. It always intrigued him, the need other cultures had for expansion, staking claim on uninhabited lands farther and farther from the port. It was something foreign to him. His people always seemed happy to just live in the lands they already had. It was the Kohtans that first introduced this need for expansion to his culture. It remained a strange, foreign concept that Thoros never felt compelled to adopt. However, unlike the people that destroyed his home, the Caldorians seemed much more peaceful in this endeavor. Settling down where there was no one around, or offering to simply join an existing encampment if they liked the area. Little by little, these camps grew into villages, and some villages into towns. All the while, he watched from the outskirts, hidden in the shadows, doing what he could to keep them safe.

Originally trying to coordinate from Tesatul, the kingdom eventually set up a military camp towards the center of the continent. This camp grew from tents and latrines to houses and barracks. The land needed a place of government, and so this encampment blossomed into a fully-established city, becoming Garadale; the secondary capital of Caldor. From here, order was maintained, soldiers sent to patrol the lands, and governing officials could meet with each other as well as the people. It gave the kingdom a place to rule from on this continent, and the people a place to go to address the governing officials, should they need to. Chronol witnessed this land of green become the start of a civilization.

Back on The Old Continent, skirmishes along the border of the two kingdoms became battles, and battles became wars. The Kohtan empire would regularly test the lines protecting Caldor, and every few decades they would grow bold enough to launch a full scale attack. Each time, the Kohtan army would push the lines that kept them at bay. Caldorian soldiers would be called from all over the kingdom to reinforce the border and push the hostiles back into their lands. Years would pass before the Kohtan's bloodlust was overridden by the instinct to survive, striking up an uneasy peace until the next time they decided to try to invade again. With every attempt the Kohtan's made, Chronol's life would quickly get much more hectic. Pulling soldiers from their posts left many places light on security, and it didn't take long for bandits and the like to try to take advantage of the situation. Sightings of The Green-Eyed Guardian always rose steadily during times of war as he did his best to keep peace in the land while the soldiers were away.

Decades passed in this way. All the while, Chronol remained the same; a soldier frozen in time, watching the world around him change while he did not. Over a century of life passed in the blink of an eye, and yet he remained, with only his four-legged companion ever at his side. He took some satisfaction in knowing he'd be around to see this world continue to grow, and that he'd play a part in keeping it safe.

12

The Collector

The capital city of Doruthan has grown in beauty and majesty over the past century. The streets bustle with even more shops trading goods from all over the kingdom and even the Risen Continent. The cobblestone streets show wear and tear from decades of use, to the point that repair crews can be found throughout the city fixing the roads. The King's Manor remains as humble as ever, staying well-maintained despite its age. It's been reinforced with steel over the years, but remains true to its humble origins. The tower of marble, stone and glass, known as The Archive, seems almost more grand than before, appearing to stretch even higher into the sky. In it, a meeting is about to take place amongst the elders.

The White Weaver Council elders summoned one of their Collectors to the council chamber; a grand hall that sits atop the tower with tall, arched ceilings and walls of glass. They sat in the center of the chamber at a long, semi-circular table where they were able to see all of Doruthan.

"I sense he's arrived," one of the elders commented. As he did, one of the tower guards entered the room, lowering his head before addressing the council.

"The Collector you summoned has arrived, sirs. What would you have me do?" the guard asked.

"Send him in, Vasrin," one of the other council members spoke up. The guard nodded and left the room.

The Collector, a young man donning the traditional, pale robes of the order, entered the chamber. He approached the inner circle of the table and knelt before the elders to await his instructions.

"Collector Oren," the center-most elder spoke up. This was the High Elder Malias, speaker of the council. His robes were trimmed in silver thread, denoting his rank among the White Weavers. "It has been brought to the council's attention that there may be an old text of some import that has surfaced recently."

"I see," Oren nodded. "What would you have me do, masters?"

"Well," Malias continued, "this is normally the part where we send a Collector to find it, validate it, and bring it back to the vault for safekeeping. However, this particular find is something of an oddity."

"How so, master?" the Collector asked.

"It seems this text surfaced on The Risen Continent…" the High Elder responded.

"That is strange indeed," Oren agreed. "There was nothing there to begin with, so where could this text have come from? If it truly is genuine, then someone must have brought it there from The Old Continent and maybe lost it."

"The thought had crossed our minds," Malias confirmed. "Nevertheless, it is possible it's simply a mistake on the part of the one who found it…"

"Or it's a trap," one of the other elders interjected.

"Yes, Brison," the High Elder responded, "it could also be a trap."

"Direct me and your wishes shall be done, masters," Oren chimed in. "Trap or not, it will be resolved."

"This is why we summoned you specifically, Oren," Malias smiled. "There is no can or cannot with you, simply a matter of how quickly it gets done. The tome is said to be in the hands of a man named Keveth in the town of Cahtri, a small settlement in the northwest portion of The Risen Continent. Find the tome, check its validity, and if it's real pay the finder and bring it back to the vault for cataloging and storage."

"It shall be done as you wish it, masters," the Collector acknowledged. "I shall leave immediately."

Accepting his task, the Collector made some quick preparations before heading out. Upon exiting The Archive, Oren was stopped by a tugging on his robe. He looked back to find little eyes peering up at him. "Where are you going?" the child asked.

"I've been assigned another item to collect. I leave for the Risen Continent immediately," the Collector responded.

"How long will you be gone?"

"It's far to the north, but shouldn't take more than a year or two. Listen to your instructor while I'm gone. I expect to see great progress from you upon my return."

"Yes, Father," the child replied.

Oren left Doruthan and traveled east through the grassy plains to the coastal city of Clarin. Passing ships of every size, he walked through the harbor. The smell of salt water filled the air around him and the sound of sailors loading their cargo echoed through the docks. He secured passage on a freighter bound for the Risen Continent. Noticing some clouds creeping over the sun, he boarded, working his way through the stacks of crates and into the belly of the ship. Down below, he conversed with a small group of travellers.

A storm brewed outside, soon making lanterns their only source of light. "So, what has you bravin' this storm to head towards the Risen Continent, friend?" one of the merchants asked as the ship rocked back and forth.

"I've been assigned a task," the Collector explained. "One only suited to people such as myself."

"One such as yourself?" another merchant asked, looking the Collector over. "Those robes look awfully familiar. You happen to be one of them Weaver folks?"

"Yes," he responded, "a White Weaver of Caldor to be precise."

"Ooo," one of them gasped playfully, "one of the EXTRA special ones, then?"

"I suppose you could say that," the Collector smiled softly.

"Well I'll be... kneel ya lanky git!" their leader shouted, elbowing one of his subordinates with a big smile on his face. "My apologies, my liege. These uncultured swine knew not the prestigious company we kept..." he said sarcastically, bowing halfway.

"There's no need for all that," the Collector laughed, "I'm merely a servant of the people, doing my part to heal those in need and protect that which needs protecting." The group laughed at this exchange, seeming to get along quickly.

"My name is Travin, by the way," the leader chimed in. "My apologies for the late introduction. These are my compatriots; Gimil, Varn, and the scrawny, uncivilized one there is Ollie." Each of them waved as they were introduced, Ollie smiling bashfully, rubbing his ribs where he'd been elbowed.

"A pleasure to make your acquaintance," the Collector smiled, reaching out and shaking Travin's hand. "So what brings all of you through the sea and the storm?"

"We're travelling merchants," he explained. "We've got some business in the Risen Continent and a few wares we'd like to find a buyer for." He reached into his pouch and pulled out a sparkling silver necklace, showing it to the Collector. "Things like this..."

"Well, that's quite a beautiful piece," the Collector commented as he examined the jewelry.

"Aye, only the finest," Travin continued. "It'd be the perfect gift to bring home to that special someone... don't you think?" he smiled.

"Thank you, friend, but I'll pass," the Collector said solemnly.

"What's the matter?" the merchant asked. "Don't tell me a handsome White Weaver of Caldor doesn't have a special woman waiting for him at home. You look a fine catch to be sure.

"Not anymore..." he responded.

"I know that face," Travin continued. "What happen'? She leave you for another man?"

"No," the Collector said quietly, "she passed on during childbirth."

"Oh..." the merchant said, realizing the mess he'd made of the conversation. "My apologies, friend... I didn't mean to bring up such memories." The room remained quiet for a few moments, an awkwardness lingering in the air. The only noise to break the silence was thunder and the creaking wood of the ship as it was jostled from side to side in the waves. The Collector closed his eyes, breathing slowly. Little by little, a soft glow began to emanate from his body. The light faded and he opened his eyes looking less sorrowful and more at peace.

"It's alright, Travin," he finally spoke up. "You didn't know. It's in the past now."

They carried on throughout the voyage, keeping each other company as the journey and the bad weather dragged on.

"Well, if they're sending you all the way across the sea from the Caldorian capital, whatever you're doing must be important," one of them commented.

"I suppose I'll find out," the Collector responded.

The storm was relentless as the ship tried to make its way across the sea. It rocked the ship with winds and rains for nearly the entire journey, finally passing just two days before the Risen Continent could be seen on the horizon. They arrived late, the month-long voyage doubled by the storm. The passengers disembarked, embraced by the warm sun they hadn't seen in what seemed like forever. They walked through the construction being done to the harbor in Tesatul, the sound of hammers and saws echoing around them.

"So, where ya' headed, lad?" Travin asked.

"My journey takes me north," the Collector responded. "A small town called Cahtri it seems."

"Well then," the merchant smiled, "it would seem a happy coincidence that we're headed to Turkdale, just east of there. What say we travel north together? These lands are still largely untamed and there's safety in numbers, don't ya' think?"

"Yes," the Collector responded, "Some company on the long road north would be nice."

They travelled for months, making their way further and further north along dirt paths and barely explored lands. The group finally arrived at the little village of Turkdale. Full of mostly farms and mills, the village was a quiet, peaceful place.

"Well, friend," Travin said, "this be our stop. You gonna be alright on your own the rest of the way?"

"I'll manage," The Collector responded. "I've gone through most of my travel supplies, but I have enough to get to my destination and back to Turkdale. I'll stop back here once I've finished my business in Cahtri. Perhaps we can grab a meal before I resupply and head home."

"That sounds like a fine idea, lad," Travin smiled, shaking his hand. "We look forward to seeing you again soon."

"Until then," the Collector waved, as he continued his journey westward.

Cahtri, a smaller farming village, wasn't far from Turkdale, and so it only took him a week to arrive. He entered a local tavern to inquire as to the location of the man he was seeking. The smell of wine and ale was in the air, the soft sound of a violin filling the room. An older gentleman sat playing his instrument in the corner near the bar, a glow and a small pillar of smoke emanated from his pipe. The Collector approached the counter and asked the barkeep about the man he was seeking, but to no avail. He looked around and saw the other patrons scattered throughout the tavern.

A pair of burly men, with black hair and beards, sat together with their pints of ale. A young woman sat at the next table, her hair as red as the wine she sipped. Further still was an old man whose hair had long since turned gray and white. His hand trembled as he carefully raised his glass to his lips. Tucked away in the corner sat a much younger man in armor, leaning back against the wall drinking water. His dog's tail was wrapped around the feet of his chair. The Collector decided to ask the others in the bar about the man he was seeking, and thankfully the young lady knew who it was from the description. The information he acquired led him to a small, worn-down house in the eastern part of town. There he located the one who had reported finding the old text.

"You must be Keveth," said Oren, happy to have apparently made it to his destination. "You're the one who reported the tome, yes?"

"Yes, Weaver," the elderly man confirmed, "that was me. I'm thankful you came all this way. It's been some time since I reported the tome, I was starting to think maybe no one was coming."

"Simply a matter of distance, sir," the Collector explained. "I left the moment I was given the order. It's quite the journey from Doruthan to here."

"Of course," the old man nodded, "my apologies. I meant no disrespect."

"None taken, sir," Oren responded politely. "May I see the piece? I'd like to take a look at it."

"Of course," Keveth nodded, "That's why you came all this way after all." He walked over to a cupboard where a parcel was wrapped with cloth. Taking it from the small shelf, he handed it to the Collector. "There she is in all her glory. I hope it was worth the trip."

Oren carefully unwrapped the cloth, exposing the old book underneath. The leather bindings were battered from age and the pages seemed old and worn. The text appeared to be references to some sort of Shadowmage experimentation. Everything he checked seemed to indicate the validity of the tome. "This is quite the find, sir. If you don't mind me asking, how exactly did you come across it?" the Collector asked.

"Well," the old man responded, looking curiously at the Weaver. "I didn't steal it if that's what you're getting at…"

"No, no," Oren assured the man, "nothing like that. I was just curious is all. It's rare to find a tome such as this so far from The Old Continent. I simply wondered what might have caused it to come into your possession. I feel the Council would be appreciative of the added detail as they too found it curious to discover such a tome so far into the new world."

"I see," Keveth nodded. "Fair enough. Was the strangest thing. I settled into this plot of land a couple years ago and I've been slowly trying to cultivate it and get some proper crops growing. However, when I was out tilling the land, I got stuck at one point. I looked to see if I was caught on a rock or something, and to my surprise what I found was the remains of a man. I was startled at first, but when I took a closer look I realized he must've been dead for some time. His body was already returning to the earth. I noticed a satchel with his body and that's where I found the book."

"I see…" the Collector nodded, listening intently to the story. "A lost Shadowmage, perhaps… interesting indeed. I can only wonder what he was doing all the way out here. Nevertheless, I appreciate the added detail and notifying us of the book's existence. We'll be sure to keep it safe going forward. Now then, all that's left is the matter of your payment."

He paid the man and thanked him again, then started heading back to Turkdale. However, as he was leaving Cahtri he found himself greeted by familiar faces.

The Collector was surprised to find his travelling merchant friends on the outskirts of town. More surprising still was the fact that they were armed. Their friendly smiles had been replaced with ominous grins. Apparently, these so-called merchants were actually thieves. When they had heard the item the Collector was retrieving would be taken to the Caldorian capital, they assumed anything worth such a journey would be worth stealing. "Come now, boy, you can't take the four of us with just your little staff. Hand us what you found and we'll let you be on your way." The Collector struck his staff down into the ground, stepped forward and stood there in silence. "Very well, it seems he wants us to take it from him, lads." As the four thieves began to approach him, the Collector raised one of his hands and wind started to swirl around them, laying the grass flat. "What's this?" one of them asked, watching the twigs at his feet fly up around them. The wind became stronger till their feet lifted off the ground.

"We Weavers call this a Whirling Vortex," the Collector finally said. The thieves spun around as if caught inside a tornado. The faster they spun, the more disoriented they became, losing grip of their weapons which flew out of the vortex.

"Did you think the council would send someone all this way, alone, to collect something they couldn't protect?" the Collector asked. He gestured his hand to the side, sending one of the thieves flying out of the vortex and into a tree, knocking him unconscious. "Consider this your Weaving lesson for the day," the Collector continued. He gestured his hand to the other side, sending another thief flying out of the vortex into a nearby boulder. "Weavers use their magical gifts to impose their will on the matter around them, changing it accordingly. In this case, you find yourselves caught in a vortex I've created, which will get faster and more violent the more magic I focus into it. Collectors are trained specifically in the combat arts of weaving, so we are more than capable of protecting whatever items we are sent to collect. That being said, the most important part of your lesson is this…" the Collector grinned, closing his hand into a fist which pulled the two remaining thieves together. Their bodies crashed into one another and fell to the ground. "Never try to steal from a Collector."

The Collector pulled his staff from the ground and began to walk away. He was stopped by a sound trailing behind him which turned out to be a trickle of water dripping from his pouch. It would appear when the thieves' weapons went flying, one of them had pierced his water pouch, spilling its contents. Realizing he wouldn't be able to make it back to Turkdale without water, he returned to Cahtri to purchase a new pouch and get more water for the journey. He went back to the tavern he'd visited previously and purchased what he needed, along with a glass of water to drink before heading back to Turkdale. The burly men from earlier were still there, new pints in hand. The young lady and old man were nowhere to be found. The young man still sat, leaning against the wall.

The Collector sat with the young man. "Do you not drink ale?" he asked. "Uncommon to find someone drinking water in a tavern like this."

The young man remained against the wall. "I've never been one for ales or wines," he responded.

"I see," said the Collector, "a man after my own heart." He reached out his hand to properly greet the man, but paused when he saw brown and silver eyes looking up at him from the floor. The tail he saw earlier belonged not to a dog, but to a wolfhound which had laid in the shadows. "That's quite a rare pet to have..." the Collector commented, "I feel as though reaching out just now might not have been the safest idea..."

The man looked over to him and shook his hand. "He knows when someone means me harm, you're safe for the time being." Reaching out, his hood tilted back, revealing his eyes.

The Collector froze, his jaw slowly dropping as a look of shock crept over his face. "It's you..." the Collector whispered. "I can't believe it's actually you..."

The man rested his head back against the wall. "I'm not sure who you think I am, Weaver, but it's unlikely we've met before," he responded.

"I see you recognize the robes of the Order," said the Collector, "Forgive me for not introducing myself properly. My name is Oren. It's true we've never met, but I've been hoping to find you for years now. The eyes and wolfhound confirm it, you must be the Green-Eyed Guardian."

"That old legend? Plenty of people have green eyes," the man said.

"True, but none glow green like a moor dragon's flame. None except for yours. I knew when I read the stories of your deeds that you had to be one of The Fallen Heroes. But where are the others?" Oren asked, looking around.

"There are no others like me. Believe me, I've looked," Chronol sighed, "I've searched for longer than you could realize and found no one."

The Collector reached into his bag and pulled out a small book. Its leather cover was worn but carefully preserved, the bindings aged and tattered from years of reading. He opened the book and gently turned its pages. "That can't be right. The Foretelling of Meera clearly states there should be a group of you," he pondered.

"What foretelling?" Chronol asked, "I've searched for over a century, there are no texts that reference what I am."

"Could it really have meant to be this long?" Oren thought out loud, seeming to not hear Chronol's statement. "I know there's supposed to be a great period of time before you find the others, but I didn't think it'd be this long," he said, continuing to flip through the pages.

"I doubt your magic book has anything in it related to me. If such a text existed, I would have found it a long time ago," Chronol said.

"This is the only text that I know of that references you, Guardian. It's unlikely you would have had access to it as it's been in The Archive for decades," the Collector said, pointing to some text on the page. "Here we are. This is the part that refers to you... It speaks of a warrior who would die in battle, but death would not hold him. 'The magic of the Earth would resurrect him, and he would leave the battlefield unscathed, but changed. The changes in him made evident by the green glow in his eyes. A man outside of time, he would long roam the land in search of more like him; others who have passed and been brought back by the magic, gathering them together until ALL SEVEN are united as one with a common purpose. Only then can they defeat the darkness that threatens to destroy all life. These timeless beings are the hope of humanity, our fate rests in the hands of these Fallen Heroes Reborn.' You see, there should be seven of you."

Chronol's expression remained unconvinced. "This sounds like something someone wrote in order to explain the origin of the Green-Eyed Guardian. When was this magic book of yours written?" Chronol asked.

Oren looked over the page, "It was written in The 76th Year of the Two Kingdoms."

Chronol's face changed from disbelief to shock. "...What year did you say?" he asked.

"The 76th Year of the Two Kingdoms," the Collector repeated, "the same year as the Bat..."

"The Battle of Thoros..." Chronol interrupted, no longer leaning against the wall. Maksis lifted his head as Chronol stared at the Collector, his face seemed almost desperate. "Please tell me more. Where did this book come from? Why do you have it? What else does it say?" he begged.

Oren calmed Chronol down and explained that the text had been in The Archive since before he was born. After accidentally stumbling upon it while exploring The Vault, Oren had found the story about The Fallen Heroes so intriguing that he kept reading it over and over. He researched and gathered whatever related information he could find elsewhere in the archive. The only documented information they had that matched the foretelling was the stories of the Green-Eyed Guardian. Eventually the Collector came to the conclusion that the Green-Eyed Guardian must be the green-eyed warrior from the foretelling. He'd been carrying the book with him ever since, hoping that his journeys as a Collector would someday bring him in contact with The Fallen Heroes.

Chronol inquired as to the others mentioned in the foretelling. "Unfortunately there isn't much information on them," the Collector responded, "It states you'd wander for some time before finally finding the first of them, but I didn't realize it meant THIS long. Sadly it doesn't explain how you'll find them."

"What is this darkness it spoke of?" asked Chronol. "Times seem pretty peaceful with the exception of thieves and bandits. It's been nearly fifty years since the Third War of Kings," he continued.

"True, but I fear that peace won't last. Between the information I've gathered from the foretelling, and some old manuscripts from the shadowmages, I think the darkness is most likely the Shadow Golem," Oren explained, "A being created by the Shadowmage Degarios, who was considered to be the most powerful shadowmage of his era. It's said that Degarios created the Shadow Golem, after years of meditation and experimentation, as a combat tool to protect him and fight for him. However, the being he created proved to be too powerful, even for Degarios, and rather than protect him, it killed him. It has remained hidden ever since, but there are shadowmage texts that warn against its return. One ancient text I read actually said the Shadow Golem has been creating things called Shayds: weaker golems created to serve the Shadow Golem and influence events throughout history."

"So their master remains hidden in the shadows, watching his plan unfold... Does it mention HOW the Shayds are affecting events?" Chronol asked.

"I'm not sure how accurate this is," the Collector responded, "I could only find one reference to the Shayds, but the text suggested they are actually possessing people. They take hold of them through the darkness in their souls and control their actions, inciting conflict, possibly even instigating the Wars of the Kings. If this is true, it would explain why the Kohtan army has been more vicious and deadly with each war. The Third War of Kings only lasted 2 years, yet they pushed farther into our lands and killed more Caldorians than in the 6 years of the previous war. What if these Shayds are possessing Kohtan soldiers and overlords to tip the scales in their favor? If this keeps up, it's only a matter of time before they control enough of the Kohtan Empire to eventually destroy Caldor."

"That's a terrifying thought..." Chronol said, scratching Maksis' head, "We can't let them get away with that, can we, Maks?" Maksis closed his eyes and moaned softly, his tail wagging gently under Chronol's chair. "Seems we're in agreement." He reached out and took the collector's hand. "Thank you, Oren. You have no idea how you've just changed my life."

"My pleasure, Guardian. It's an honor to finally meet you," he responded.

"Please, call me Chronol."

"Really? So THAT's your name. I'm honored you'd share it with me,"

Oren smiled.

"It's the first time I've said it out loud in over a century. You've given this new life of mine a whole new purpose; it seems only right that you know my name." Chronol grinned.

They carried on for hours sharing stories of their adventures. Finally, it was time for them to go their separate ways; however, neither of them would forget the friend they made that day and the difference they made in each other's lives.

The Collector headed back to Doruthan, a smile on his face and his faith in the future renewed.

"Chronol would continue to wander, but this time with a purpose in mind. He would find the others like him, unite them, and save this world from the coming darkness…"

That should cover everything. I'm currently working with a couple artists on cover art for the book. What's the timetable on that so I know how hard to push them for results?

Joey Cardona is available for interviews and personal appearances. For more information contact us at info@advbooks.com

To purchase additional copies of these books, visit our bookstore at:
www.advbookstore.com

Longwood, Florida, USA
"we bring dreams to life"™
www.advbookstore.com